Title: Bad, Better than Worst.

Author: S.K.

Published by: Self published

Printed by: online publication.

First Edition: 2025

ISBN Number: 978-93-344-4766-8

श्री

I begin by bowing down to the Almighty, Thy divine essence as Creator, Preserver, and Destroyer: manifested through Brahma, Vishnu, and Mahesh. It is by Thy grace that this endeavor has taken form, and through Thy wisdom that it finds meaning.

I would like to extend my heartfelt gratitude to my godfather, my mentor, my teacher. His unwavering guidance, profound wisdom, and boundless compassion continue to illuminate my path. Though he is no longer with us in form, his spirit lives on in every word and thought that shaped this work.

I also extend my deepest thanks to all those who made this journey a safe. Every step taken was steadied by your care, every challenge met with your unwavering belief, and to every soul who offered support in countless ways. Your kindness, encouragement, and presence have been the pillars upon which this work stands.

And finally, my greatest thanks to the readers—for your time, your attention, and your willingness to walk this path with me. Your presence gives this work its true purpose.

1. Karma revolves

The script of our life is pre – written long before our first breath but the path towards this destiny is changeable by our karma. While the major themes and life events are fixed, a person's actions and intentions dictate how they navigate that preordained journey. A portion of one's accumulated karma from past lives is designated for the current life. This is known as *prarabdha karma*, or "destiny." We embark on the journey of life, traversing the path that unfolds before us, one step at a time. The road ahead, though uncertain, is not the only one available to us; our actions determine which path we would walk on, through easy or the difficult route. The path we walk reflects our values and character. We walk; driven by the winds of destiny, our feet carrying us forward, even as our heart ponder the mysteries of the universe.

In this existential odyssey, choices seem to fade away, living us with a sole option of surrendering to the present moment. Like stars swallowed by the morning sky. We wander through corridors of uncertainty, where every fork in the path dissolves into mist.

The illusion of control crumbles, leaving us with the quiet truth. Yet we dive at the best options available only to make life worth it, but sometime we are surrounded by circumstances that demand hard decisions, one which can be termed as 'BAD' decision. Though, you know that it is better than the 'WORST' alternative. At times, life corners us into situations where the luxury of a "good" choice simply doesn't exist. In such moments, we are forced to weigh the lesser of two evils, knowing that even the "bad" path spares us from the devastation of the "worst." These decisions may leave us uneasy, but they also reflect our ability to act with pragmatism rather than paralysis. Often, history and personal growth are shaped not by ideal choices, but by the strength to endure difficult ones. What matters is not that the decision was flawless, but that it prevented greater harm and allowed us to keep walking toward better possibilities.

Choosing the "bad" option doesn't mean failure–it means survival, resilience, and the courage to move forward despite imperfect circumstances.

A bad decision doesn't make you a bad person; it doesn't define one's character, instead it shapes you like a weathered stone. The future, a tapestry woven from the threads of karma and circumstances, awaits us, its secret hidden until we arrive at the threshold of tomorrows.

As I reflect on the intricate tapestry of my life, I've come to realize that karma is an unforgiving force that revolves around itself, weaving a narrative that's both predestined and influenced by the cumulative karmas of my past, present and even those of my ancestor's. It spares no one, circling back with precision, reminding us that every action—no matter how small—casts ripples that eventually return. In its relentless cycle, karma teaches that choices are not isolated threads, but knots that bind us to consequences we cannot escape. It is neither cruel nor kind, only just—an eternal mirror reflecting the truths we try to hide. The more I try to outrun it, the more I find myself entangled in the very patterns I once ignored. Perhaps this is the essence of life's design: that we are both the weavers and the woven, architects of our own fate.

There was a time when I questioned the universe seeking answers to the trials and tribulations that befell me. But now with the benefits of hindsight and a deeper understanding of the karmic forces at play, I come to accept the reasons behind the twist and turns of my journey. Perhaps, I've even glimpses of the contours of my future.

My story begins with the brave, kind and wise man, my father. As the eldest daughter I had the privilege of witnessing his selflessness and courage through the narratives of my grandfather. One incident, in particular, left an indelible mark on our family's history. My father's cousin had fallen deeply in love with a young man from a different cast, union that was forbidden in those days. When they decided to elope, the village elders and family members were outraged.

My father, determine to protect his cousin and her lover, embarked on the perilous search mission, racing against time to find them before the villagers could met out their own brand of justice. His bravery and quick thinking ultimately lead to their safe return, but the ordeal was far from over.

The village Council, fueled by traditions and prejudice, decreed that the couple could not get married. My father, aware of the devastating consequences this would have on his cousin's life, refused to accept their decision. With his educational background, government position and unwavering conviction, he stood up to the council, ultimately securing the couples right to marry.

However, there happiness was shot–lived. Tragedy struck just a year later, when the young man succumbed to pneumonia. My father was devastated, and the village, still steeped in superstitions, blamed my aunt for her husband's untimely demise.

As the villager's curses and accusation intensified, my father knew he had to act. He arranged for his sister to be remarried, despite her initial reluctance, and ensured her safety and well– being.

But she being truly committed to her love kept refusing to remarry, living no choice to my father, but to force her into this deal.

Finally the marriage did take place and she was sent away with a man ten years older to her and with this my fate was sealed.

'Destiny's dark brush strokes painted a portrait of love,

Framed with poison.

I shall witness fate's cruel hand snatching away the heart

That beats for me,

From the ashes of heartache

A phoenix of love shall rise

Radiant and strong illuminating the path to forever.'

My father's well—intended decision though rooted in a desire to protect his sister, ultimately led to her forced marriage. This pattern was destined to repeat itself, as he too was forced into the union he didn't choose. The complexities of these relationships are a testament to the enduring powers of tradition and the sacrifices made in its name.

The history repeats itself unless and until justice is served.

2. Unboxing the latest version of feelings.

"Why there are no participants from 9th B class?" the teacher literally shouted at us. There was a spelling bee competition in the school and our class, as usual, was slacking off wondering that our English teacher, Miss. Cutto was absent that day. It was mutually agreed by all the students of our class that it's a free period. So all the kids were busy gossiping, laughing, and chit chatting when suddenly she furiously appeared in the class like a genie from his lantern. Not to grant us any wish but to dictate her command.

She was Bright and Beautiful with short hair and height. When the class stood up to greet her, she could be seen by nobody. Yet she was very strict and was respectful too. We shifted uncomfortably in our seats, pretending to be busy with our notebooks.

The truth was obvious–there had been a spelling bee competition, and once again, our class had managed to dodge it. We had convinced ourselves it didn't matter. Now, with the teacher's glare fixed on us, the weight of our absence hung heavier than any word we might have had to spell.

She murmured to herself with raised eyebrows and then pointing towards me and three other girls, declared "follow me to the competition hall". We were left with no choice but to be the part of embracement at the competition.

We had no idea as what kind of spellings would be asked. Whether science, literature, Geography or how many syllable words would we asked. I tried not to lose my cool. Though I was irritated for selecting me for the competition against my will, I must admit it felt less like an honor and more like being a goat dragged to a beauty pageant. One moment I was minding my own business, happily invisible, and the next— bam! I was the 'chosen one,' except without the magical prophecy or cool sword. My classmates cheered as if I'd won the lottery, while I stood there wondering if I could trade my ticket for a nap instead. Truly, destiny has a wicked sense of humor.

I tried to stay calm which was my specialty. My friends used to say that it's not important whether I am present or absent in the class because I was no fun. I didn't speak even a single word while in the class. I was the quiet one, but for my friends, I was the boring one, which I didn't care much, because as for me – it's better to be quiet than to show your stupidity through your nonsense talk like the others do.

My friends only liked me because of my long, thick hair, fair skin and they would often compliment me for having pretty face. Basically, I was a walking combo of a fairness cream ad and a shampoo commercial. They'd say, "You're so beautiful!" and I'd smile, wondering if they'd still like me if I showed up bald, tanned, and wearing a dinosaur onesie.

Spoiler: probably not.

Turns out, friendship was just a beauty pageant with snacks. And I? I was the unwilling contestant who didn't even sign up. It was very clear, my friends adore me for my '3Hs': Hair, Hue and Hotness —not for my Harvard—smart brain (that deserved better friends to know its worth, just kidding.)

We entered the competition room. Being the latecomer's we had missed the introduction. I kept my head down till I saw my other classmates settling down on last benches.

I sat next to my best friend, the certified chatterbox of our class. If talking were an Olympic sport, she'd have a shelf full of gold medals and a fan club cheering her on. From the moment she walked into the classroom, her mouth was in motion — commenting on the weather, the teacher's outfit, the mystery of math homework, and even the existential crisis of cafeteria food. She could easily win a competition for nonstop talking, and probably host it too. She believed she was the smartest person in the room—always ready with an answer, even when no question was asked. Her confidence was unmatched, her logic... questionable.

But despite her questionable facts and wild theories, she had a charm that made it impossible to stay annoyed. Her stories, though often inaccurate, were wildly entertaining. She could turn a trip to the stationery shop into an epic saga involving lost pens, dramatic price negotiations, and a heroic escape from glitter glue.

Sitting next to her was never boring. It was like being on a rollercoaster of words—fast, unpredictable, and slightly dizzying. And while she might not have been the brightest bulb in the box, she lit up the room in her own chaotic, hilarious way.

She never required any specific topic but could go on and on for hours telling stories about anything she could possibly think about. We had exact opposite characteristics.

She always had the inside scoop on the top students of the school—especially the handsome ones. It was as if she had a secret subscription to the "Elite Boys Weekly," complete with updates on their grades, their sports achievements, their latest haircuts, and who they were rumored to be crushing on. If someone so much as sneezed in the direction of a popular guy, she'd know about it before the tissue hit the floor.

Her obsession with school royalty was unmatched. She could recite their roll numbers, their favorite subjects, and even their preferred lunchbox contents. She knew everything about them. Their addresses, their financial status, what cars their parents drove, and even where their moms bought groceries. It was like she had a personal database of elite student profiles, updated weekly with fresh gossip and insider info. If one of them moved houses, she'd know before the moving truck arrived.

And when it came to the handsome ones, her radar was sharper than a hawk's. She'd spot a new haircut from across the corridor; decode the meaning behind a raised eyebrow. Her commentary was relentless, hilarious, and oddly impressive. While the rest of us struggled to remember our own schedules, she had a mental database of every top performer's GPA, extracurricular, and emotional status. And while academic brilliance wasn't exactly her strong suit, she had a genius—level talent for gossip and decoding teenage drama, an uncanny knack for gathering intel—especially when it came to the top students. Her grades might have hovered in the "needs improvement" zone, but her knowledge of the school's social hierarchy was encyclopedic. She could tell you who topped the last math test, which got selected for the debate team, and—most importantly—who among the high achievers had the best jawline. Her priorities were crystal clear.

She once told me about a boy she had a massive crush on. And when I say she knew everything about him, I mean *everything*. His full address, his birthdate, his blood group, the name of his dog, and even the brand of toothpaste he used. But what really blew my mind was the family hierarchy she laid out like a royal lineage.

She even knew which room he slept in, which side of the bed he preferred, and what time he usually left for school. At one point, I genuinely wondered if she lived with them. Maybe she had a secret tunnel connecting her house to his, or perhaps she moonlighted as their family historian.

I asked her once, half—joking, “Are you sure you’re not part of their household?” She just laughed and whispered dramatically, as if revealing state secrets, “No, silly. I just observe things.” Observe? She was practically running a surveillance operation.

I’d blink, wondering how she even knew that. “I have sources,” she’d say with a wink.

The competitions began and first round was timer based. Each group had to answer correct spelling within 10 seconds. We were as prepared as kindergarteners for a PhD defense. The questions were easier than a Google search, but our brains decided to stage a collective protest. We spelled 'cat' as 'cta', 'dog' as 'dgo'. It was like we had a personal vendetta against the alphabet. Every letter we touched turned into a crime scene. The judge's faces were mix of confusion and horror and mild concern for our education. We scored whopping 5 points— 4 of which were probably sympathy points. And so on the competition got over within half an hour. We didn't just lose the spelling bee; we got 'bee—utifully' destroyed.

The Blame game began, each one from our group started blaming one other for being present that day. I literally wished if I could get the power to be invisible. Not to escape the room. Just to vanish from the memory of everyone who witnessed our spelling massacre. It was such a shame. Our spelling egos were crying in a corner "why? Brain, why?" Even the alphabet looked disappointed. And us? We were just trying to remember how to spell "embarrassment."

The teacher announced the winner group. As I glanced up with curiosity to see who had emerged victorious, our eyes met in a sudden sparkling connection and to my surprise, he was already staring at me. His gaze locked intensely on mine. In such a classic "caught staring" move, our eyes met for a fleeting instant and then in a perfect synchrony, we both hastily looked away, each pretending the other didn't exist. As if the brief connection had never occurred.

I stared at the floor like it owed me an explanation. My heart? Doing cartwheels. My brain? Filing a complaint titled *"Unnecessary Eye Contact in Public Spaces."* Around me, the classroom erupted in claps and cheers, but I barely heard it. I was too busy pretending to be deeply fascinated by the texture of my desk. He, on the other hand, had suddenly developed a lifelong interest in the ceiling.

A sudden, sharp, cold sensation seemed to seep into my very bones, sending shiver down my spine. My heart skipped a bit not out of fear, but something far stranger. Butterflies stirred in my stomach, not the gentle flutter of nerves, but a wild, winged storm of anticipation. I struggled to make sense of the unfamiliar, thrilling and exhilarating sensation that had taken hold of me, like nothing I had ever experienced before. It was as if the air itself had shifted, as if time had paused to whisper, "This moment matters." My thoughts scattered like stars, and for a heartbeat, I wasn't sure if I was falling in love, or falling into something far deeper — a destiny I hadn't yet dared to name.

Normally, when I caught a boy staring at me; I'd feel a surge of annoyance. Like, hello sir, do you mind? I'm trying to exist in peace. My brain would instantly activate "defensive glare mode." Eyebrows raised, Jaw clenched. The classic "Do I look like a museum exhibit?" expression because let's be honest — I wasn't flattered. I was visibly irritated.

Growing up, the boys in our class had been like brothers to me, loud, clumsy, occasionally annoying—but harmless. I had never encouraged them to think of me in any other way. I had built walls around myself making it clear that I wasn't interested in entanglements. Just me, my goals and a quiet kind of peace. But this time something felt different. His gaze didn't felt like a challenge. It felt like a question. Not the kind you answer with words, but the kind that lingers in your mind long after the moment has passed.

In the embarrassed moment like —losing the competition, the sting of failure still fresh—I should've been sulking. But instead, I found myself smiling. Not because it didn't hurt, but because, somehow, in the middle of all that awkwardness, I felt a spark of connection that I couldn't ignore. It was as if he had awakened a part of me that I never knew existed. His gaze had made me felt noticed. Like I am “someone's special someone”. As if I found something way better than what I lost. It was a spark. A beginning. A quiet kind of magic that whispered, “You matter. To me.”

Meanwhile, the teacher instructed the rest of the group to return to their respective classes. I stepped out of the competition room. My mind looming on the mysterious stranger. Despite the undeniable connection we had shared, I was left with the nagging sense of uncertainty. I knew nothing about him, not even his name.

It was strange, really. How someone could occupy so much space in your thoughts without ever uttering a word. I had built a version of him in my mind, pieced together from fragments—a tilt of the head, the way he tapped his fingers when he was deep in thought, the books he carried, the way he looked out the window as if searching for something beyond the horizon. But it was all guesswork, a mosaic of impressions without a single fact to anchor it.

I found myself wondering: Who was he, really? What did he dream about? What made him laugh? Did he even notice me the way I noticed him? The mystery was both thrilling and maddening. It was like reading the first chapter of a novel and never getting to turn the page.

And so, I sat with that ache of curiosity, that quiet longing to know more. Because sometimes, the most powerful connections are the ones that remain undefined—beautiful in their ambiguity, haunting in their incompleteness.

As an introvert, I found myself hesitant to ask my friends about the mysterious stranger. It wasn't that I didn't want to know—I did, desperately—but the thought of voicing my curiosity felt like stepping into a spotlight I wasn't ready for. My comfort zone had always been the quiet corners, the unnoticed glances, the silent observations from afar. I was the kind of person who watched stories unfold rather than star in them. My natural tendency to observe from the distance worn out but I couldn't bring myself to cross that invisible line between wondering and knowing and I choose to keep my curiosity locked away. Silent enquiry being a safer option than risking vulnerability. And maybe that's the thing about being an introvert—you feel everything deeply, but you carry it quietly. You build entire stories in your head, hoping that someday, somehow, the world will read between the lines.

But the world rarely does.

It moves too fast, too loud, too distracted to notice the silent poetry unfolding behind your eyes. So you learn to treasure your inner world, to find comfort in the quiet corners of your mind where your thoughts can breathe freely. You become fluent in the language of glances, in the subtle art of observation, in the unspoken connections that flicker like candlelight between people who may never speak.

You watch others live out loud—bold, expressive, unafraid—and you wonder what it might feel like to be that open, that seen. But then you remember: your silence isn't emptiness. It's depth. It's the space where your imagination blooms, where your emotions echo, where your truths take root.

And maybe, one day someone will pause long enough to notice. To listen. To read between the lines and find the story you've been writing all along.

As the days turned into weeks, my thoughts of him began to fade—slowly, like the dying echoes of sound in a mountain valley, lingering just long enough to remind me they were once loud and clear. What had once felt like a spark of something meaningful now drifted into the background of my everyday life, blurred by routine and swallowed by silence. His identity remained elusive, like a name half–remembered in a dream, just out of reach no matter how hard I tried to grasp it.

Despite my curiosity, I couldn't shake off the feeling that finding him was a lost cause. It was as if the universe had designed our encounter to be fleeting–a moment suspended in time, beautiful in its brevity, frustrating in its incompleteness. I had no clues, no connections; no reason to believe our paths would cross again. And yet, a part of me still searched for him in crowded hallways, in quiet classrooms, in the faces of strangers who bore a passing resemblance.

But eventually, I stopped looking. Not out of indifference, but out of acceptance. Some stories aren't meant to be finished. Some people are meant to remain mysteries. And the magic of that moment lay in its uncertainty–in the not knowing, in the wondering, in the quiet ache of what could have been.

One day, while I was sitting with my classmates, lost in the usual rhythm of chatter and notebooks, I noticed a boy standing just outside our classroom door. He wasn't moving, just standing there—his gaze fixed on me with a quiet intensity that made my heart skip. It wasn't threatening, but it was deliberate, curious, like he was trying to memorize something about me without saying a word.

I tried to act normal, pretending not to notice, but my thoughts were racing. Who was he? Why was he looking at me like that?

Moments later, one of my classmates leaned in and whispered, "That boy outside... he's asking about you." His voice was low, almost conspiratorial, and I felt a strange mix of surprise and unease. Apparently, he had asked for my name, but my classmate—bless his loyalty—had chosen to protect my privacy. He told him only that I was a good person and that he shouldn't bother me.

I didn't know whether to feel grateful or disappointed. A part of me was curious—desperately so. Why me? What did he want? But another part of me, the quieter, more cautious part, was relieved that the moment had passed without confrontation.

He lingered for a few more seconds, then turned and walked away; leaving behind a trail of questions I couldn't answer. And just like that, the classroom returned to its usual hum.

The next day another girl from my class approached me with the curious expression "A boy from next class is asking about you." She said. "I've already told him your name. Do you know him?" She looked at me expectantly waiting for my response.

I hesitantly turned around to see who that boy was inquiring about me every day. To my astonishment, when I looked at him I realized that he was the mysterious stranger from spelling bee competition. I jumbled with confusion, irritation and excitement. And for a moment, it felt like the universe had pulled a prank on me. *Of all people... him?* Suddenly, the spelling bee disaster didn't feel so disastrous. Because maybe, just maybe, I hadn't lost that day. I'd just stumbled into the beginning of a story I never saw coming.

I couldn't help but feel a thrill at the thought of him going to such a great length to find me.

I pretended not to notice him, ignoring his very existence. But deep down I was thrilled to discover that he was making an effort to learn about me. Me, the girl who had mastered the art of emotional invisibility.

I had thought I was the only one feeling this way but now that I know he was just as invested. Seeing him stand outside, asking about me every day, doubled my excitement. I felt a sense of relief to understand that I didn't have to make the first move – something I might never ever had done otherwise also. Instead I could sit back, relax and see how things unfolded it was like watching a fascinating episode wondering what he would come up with next

That night I went into overdrive. Sleep? Who needs sleep when you are trying to guess a mysterious admirer? My brain was like a sports commentator "And now he's got my name, he's got my class, what's his next play?" Will he accidentally bump into me in the hallway? Coincidentally follow me home and claim he's just really into my neighborhood's architecture? Or will he go full – on ninja and ambush me with his small talk? I spent entire night thinking about this and that, running over all the possibilities.

Next day while entering my school, I couldn't brush of the feeling that I was being watched and not in a creepy, 'I'm— being— stalked— by— a secret –admirer' kind of a way, all though that did turn out to be partially true. No, this was more like 'I— am— being— orchestrated – by— a— mysterious— force' kind of feeling.

Little did I know my life was about to take a dramatic turn. courtesy of a mysterious figure who would stop at nothing to... well, not exactly win my heart but more like reveal shocking truth that would leave me speechless.

The excuse he came up with was far—fetched so beyond my wildest imagination, that I would have never ever in a million years thought it possible. I mean who comes up with the stuff like this.

'Hey guess what? We are relatives'. Yeah, because that's exactly what I wanted to hear from a guy who's been secretly admiring me. For this was his real excuse. Not "I like you." Not "You're different." but *relatives*. Like fate took one look at my love life and said, "Let's make this awkward." Suddenly, every stolen glance, every lingering smile — rewritten by the family tree and I stood there, blinking, trying to decide whether to laugh, cry, or call a genealogist.

My friend approached me with a curious expression again, “Hey you won't believe what he just told Me.” she said containing her excitement. “He says, you two are related and he wants to meet up with you to discuss... something.” I was taken aback to say the list. My mind was racing with questions. What kind of relative? Distance cousin? Long — lost sibling? And what did he want to talk to me about? Was it a family reunion? An inheritance? A secret family recipe?

My thoughts raced, colliding with each other in a whirlwind of possibilities. I tried to recall every family gathering, every story my parents had ever told me, every name that had floated through conversations like forgotten whispers. Nothing, no clue. Just a blank space where answers should have been.

I glanced toward the boy outside the classroom. He was still there, standing with a quiet patience that made the moment feel even more surreal. There was no urgency in his posture, no sign of discomfort — just a calm, steady gaze that seemed to be waiting for something. For me.

A part of me wanted to walk out and ask him directly. Another part hesitated, wary of the unknown. What did he want to discuss? Why now? And why me?

I turned back to my classmate, hoping for more details, but she simply shrugged. "He didn't say much. Just that it's important."

Important. That word settled heavily in my chest. Whatever this was, it wasn't casual. And whether I was ready or not, it seemed like the past — or perhaps a hidden part of it — was knocking on my door.

I was skeptical. Related? Really? But at the same time I was curious. What could he possibly want to talk to me about? Love? Nah, relatives don't talk about love things. They talk in half—sentences and full judgments. Maybe this mysterious relative of mine had a story to tell that would change my life forever or maybe he just wanted to borrow some sugar because in this family, life—altering revelations and grocery requests arrive with the same level of suspense. He looked at me like he held galaxies behind his eyes. I looked at him like I hoped

he'd brought his own spoon. And in that moment, the air shimmered –
not with magic, but with the possibility of either a prophecy... or pancakes.

Either way, I refused to meet up. I needed to borrow some more time to understand myself first. To untangle the knots of curiosity and confusion that tightened with every passing thought. This wasn't just about meeting a stranger who claimed to be a relative. It was about facing a part of me I hadn't yet come to understand. I wanted to unravel my feelings, process my thoughts and gain clarity on my emotions before diving into this unexpected twist.

There was something sacred about that pause – about choosing introspection over impulse. I didn't want to be swept away by someone else's story before I had fully grasped my own.

So I stayed still. I let the questions simmer. I allowed the silence to speak. And in that quiet space, I began to listen—not to the voices around me, but to the one within me. The one that had always been there, waiting patiently to be heard.

I decided to ignore him for the time being and focus on my personal growth. At my age, I wasn't interested in pursuing romantic relationship. And I certainly didn't want to risk damaging my reputation at school. My safety, stability and personal value was crucial to me. So I chose to maintain my boundaries and stay true to myself.

I resigned and before I knew it, the ninth grade had drawn to a close. I found myself standing on the threshold of a pivotal moment, the pressure packed Tenth – grade.

3. Love lockdown.

Today marks the first day of an extravagantly crucial academic year one for which we have been meticulously groomed, rigorously trained and even disciplined with unyielding fervor — no matter the tool, be it a stick or a rolling pin or Mom's sandal. The mighty tenth grade had begun.

The air in school felt different. Heavier. As if the walls themselves knew we were now tenth graders and expected us to act accordingly. No more doodling in notebooks, no more sneaky naps during history. We were now part of the elite squad—the board exam battalion. Our names would soon be etched into school records, our marks dissected at dinner tables, and our futures speculated upon by relatives we hadn't seen in years.

And yet, beneath all the seriousness, there was a strange thrill. A sense of stepping into something big. Something that would challenge us, shapes us, and maybe even breaks us a little — only to rebuild us stronger.

So here we are. Pens sharpened, minds alert, hearts pounding. The tenth grade has arrived, and we're ready to face it – armed with determination, a stack of notebooks, and the lingering sting of Mom's sandal as a reminder that failure is not an option.

I stepped into the classroom, expecting the usual hum of chatter and the comforting rhythm of routine. But instead, I was met with a surprise announcement that instantly shifted the air. The teacher, with a tone that was both formal and final, declared that I – along with two of my friends – was being transferred to a new class.

Not just any class.

This was the class whispered about in corridors, the one that carried a reputation like a crown and a curse. It was notoriously more challenging, filled with the school's top performers–the ones who solved math problems before the teacher finished writing them, who spoke in fluent scientific jargon, and who treated exams like friendly sparring matches.

My heart sank and soared at the same time. Part of me felt honored, as if we'd been chosen for something elite.

But another part of me panicked. Was I ready for this? Could I keep up? Would I belong?

My friends exchanged wide—eyed glances, their expressions mirroring my own mix of excitement and dread. We were being uprooted from our comfort zone and dropped into a world of fierce competition and relentless expectations. The classroom we were leaving had been our safe haven—familiar faces, inside jokes, and a rhythm we understood. The one we were entering felt like stepping into a storm.

As we gathered our things and prepared to move, I couldn't help but wonder: Was this a test of our potential or a push into the deep end? Both way, the journey had begun — and there was no turning back.

With each step down the corridor, my anxiety grew. I had spent years cultivating friendship and sense of security only to be uprooted in the final year of school. The daunting prospect of starting a new in a high—achieving class, surrounded by unfamiliar faces and expectations left me wondering: How would I survive? Who would I turn to? As an average student, with grades hovering around 65 to 70%, I felt like a small fish in a vast uncharted ocean. As I entered into the new classroom, the welcome was far from warm. The room was filled with students who seemed utterly indifferent to our presence. No smiles, no curious glances, just a sea of apathetic faces. I felt a sting of insecurity. Like an unwelcomed guest crashing a party.

The teacher's finger jabbed toward the last bench where a single vacant spot seemed to be waiting just for me. "Sit there" she said, her tone neutral. I made my way to the back of the classroom, feeling like a temporary guest and settled into the empty space trying to blend in and avoid drawing attention to myself.

I slid into the seat, its wooden surface cool against my palms, etched with the ghosts of names and doodles from students past. A constellation of ink stains and scratches whispered silent stories—of boredom, rebellion, maybe even brilliance. I traced one with my finger absentmindedly, a jagged heart pierced by an arrow, initials faded but still clinging to the grain.

Around me, the classroom buzzed with the low hum of chatter and shifting chairs. No one looked back. Or maybe they did, in those sideways glances that vanish the moment you try to meet them. I kept my eyes on the desk, on the chipped edge of the bench, on anything but the sea of unfamiliar faces.

The teacher's voice resumed a steady rhythm of instruction that washed over me like distant thunder. I tried to listen, but the words blurred, tangled in the knots of my own thoughts. What did they already know? What had I missed? Would I always feel like a shadow in someone else's story?

A breeze slipped through the open window, stirring the edge of my notebook. I caught it before it fluttered away, anchoring it with my elbow. Outside, a crow cawed once–sharp, solitary. I envied its certainty, its place in the sky.

The teacher finished taking attendance and began to explain the first lesson of the first day. I tried to focus but my attention kept wavering as I noted that I am being watched intently by the side bencher. I felt like a prisoner trapped in a cell, unable to muster the courage to glance up and identify the person staring at me. So I resorted to a defensive strategy. Concealed by self–consciousness, I pretended being lost in my books to avoid further scrutiny.

I flipped a page I hadn't read, letting the rustle of paper mask my unease. My fingers gripped the edges of the textbook like it was a shield, though the words blurred into meaningless shapes. The classroom around me felt distant, like a stage play I wasn't cast in—just a silent observer tucked into the wings.

The side bencher's gaze was relentless. I could feel it like a spotlight on my skin, tracing the outline of my presence. Every movement I made—adjusting my collar, tucking a strand of hair—felt exaggerated, exposed. I wondered if anyone else noticed, or if I was the only one caught in this quiet standoff.

The teacher's voice droned on, a monotone rhythm that barely pierced the fog in my mind. Something about integers. Something about rules. But all I could think about was the weight of that stare, and the question it carried: *Why me?*

The classes seemed to be endless, with each teacher's arrival and departure, the inferiority within me seemed to be only intensifying. At last, the moment I had been waiting for, since the dawn of eternity, arrived. The last bell's chime echoing through the halls, declaring the end of the day.

To my greatest surprise, for the first time in my whole life I realized that the school bell had such an immense power, the power to make you strong and bold that you can walk fearlessly straight out of the very class, where earlier you were afraid of even stepping in. The school bell rang – not like a dull clang, but like a trumpet of triumph. Suddenly, I wasn't the nervous newcomer clutching my notebook like a lifeline. I was a warrior of the last period, striding out of the classroom like I owned the hallway. The same room that had swallowed me whole now seemed like a conquered kingdom. My steps were bold. My backpack swung with swagger. The corridor lights seemed to flicker in applause. I even nodded at the side bencher – yes, that one, like we were old allies in a secret mission.

The bell had done it. It had cast a spell of courage, a charm of exit–stage–left confidence. I imagined it had a secret name: *Liberatus Maximus*.

And as I walked out, I whispered to myself, "Next time, I'll enter like this too."

I reached home with the weight of a thousand textbooks pressing on my soul. Not physically, of course–my bag was light. But emotionally? I was dragging a whole syllabus of anxiety behind me.

Tomorrow, I'd have to sit in that same class again. That same bench. That same side bencher with the X–ray vision. I could already hear the teacher's voice echoing in my head: *"Open your books to page 1."* Page 1? I hadn't even emotionally recovered from page 0.

I flopped onto my bed like a tragic heroine in a school–themed soap opera. My pillow absorbed my sigh like a seasoned therapist. I stared at the ceiling, hoping it would offer me a transfer certificate to another dimension.

My mom peeked in: "How was your first day?"

I considered replying in interpretive dance—something between a slow collapse and a dramatic faint—but settled for a groan that translated roughly to *"I survived, but barely, I got transferred into new class."*

Great. Now I had mystery, suspense, and social pressure. This wasn't school—it was a psychological thriller.

I rolled over, pulled the blanket over my head, and whispered to the universe: "Dear tomorrow, be gentle. Or at least bring snacks."

I sighed so deeply even before getting out of my bed. The morning sun seemed to be announcing the start of the war. Today is the second day and I have to get ready to face the next challenges about which I don't even have any idea what it could be.

The battle ahead weighted heavily on my mind. Just then a tempting thought popped into my head. "Should I skip school today?" But I quickly dismissed the idea, knowing my mother would never permit it. Her mantra echoed in my mind "No skipping classes". So I threw off the covers and began getting ready for the challenges ahead.

I reached school like a lone warrior returning from exile, greeting every pebble and stone on the path like old comrades. I knew no human would greet me in that class, so I made peace with the gravel. At least they didn't judge my hairstyle.

In the corridor, I stumbled upon old friends–those legendary beings who once shared my lunch and my secrets, and occasionally my homework answers. We exchanged warm glances, the kind that say, "We survived last year's math teacher. We can survive anything." No words were needed. Just a silent nod, a raised eyebrow, and a mutual understanding: we were still alive, still awkward, and still fabulous.

As I tiptoed into the new class like a spy entering enemy territory, bracing for the cold silence of unfamiliar faces and the smell of fresh notebooks, I heard a gentle voice call my name. "Good morning!" it chirped, like a sunbeam wrapped in kindness. I turned, eyes wide, heart doing cartwheels. Was this a trap? A prank? A hallucination brought on by too much homework?

But no—it was real. A human. A kind one. Possibly magical. I gazed at her with big bright eyes, like a squirrel spotting a nut after winter. The joy was overwhelming. The shadows of loneliness melted like butter on a hot paratha. I smiled so hard my cheeks filed a complaint.

And just like that, the day transformed. The classroom didn't feel like a dungeon anymore. It felt like a stage. And I was ready to perform.

As the classroom filled up, the atmosphere transformed into a sunny bright smiles which greeted me welcome, revealing the humble and kind nature of my new classmates. Receiving such comfort boosted my confidence giving me a renewed sense of purpose.

A week passed by, and just when we thought we'd finally memorized the exact angle to avoid eye contact during surprise quizzes, our teacher dropped a bombshell. With the solemnity of a royal decree, she stood before us and announced:

"A new sitting arrangement will be implemented. Students shall rotate seats every alternate day."

The class fell silent. You could hear the collective gasp of introverts echoing off the walls.

Suddenly, our front–benchers—those brave souls who had willingly sacrificed their eyesight for academic glory—looked betrayed. The back–benchers, meanwhile, exchanged high–fives like they'd just won the lottery. "Finally, I shall taste the forbidden fruit of legroom and proximity to the fan."

Chaos ensued. Calculators were whipped out to predict future seat positions. Alliances were formed. "Swap with me on Thursday and I'll give you my extra tiffin on

Monday," someone bartered. It was like chess, but with pencil boxes and emotional damage.

And then came the real twist: the teacher added, "This will help you all mingle and learn from each other."

Learn? From each other? We barely remembered each other's names beyond roll numbers and lunchbox smells.

Still, the rule was law. And so began the Great Migration—every alternate day, a new view, a new neighbor, and a fresh existential crisis. The only constant? The teacher's amused smile as she watched us scramble like musical chairs with a side of mild panic.

My peace of mind was bombarded within a fraction of seconds. The level of difficulties was only getting higher. Each day new partner means new kind of awkwardness. Everybody was unhappy with this rule. But nobody had power to change it, so we had no other option but to nod our head in acceptance.

With each new partnership, on each succeeding day, the classroom became a kaleidoscope of connections. Adaptability flourished, creativity flooded and it had a surprisingly positive impact on our learning.

However, I must admit that there was one aspect that made me slightly uncomfortable – being paired with a boy. The initial awkwardness was undeniable. I sat down like I was entering a diplomatic summit. He nodded. I nodded. We both stared at our notebooks like they were escape routes. But as we worked together, I realized that it helped me break out of my shell and interact with someone known as topper of the class.

He was calm. Too calm. Like the kind of calm that makes you wonder if he's secretly meditating while solving equations. And shy – so shy that when he said "Hi," it felt like a rare Pokémon had spoken. Despite of initial hesitation, I grew to appreciate the experience and awkwardness gave way to understanding. Turns out, being paired with the calmest, shyest topper wasn't a punishment.

I had set my target. Seventy percent. Not seventy—one. Not seventy—two. Seventy. It was my Everest, my moon landing, my personal "Mission Possible."

I crafted a daily timetable with the precision of a NASA engineer. 6:00 AM: Wake up. 6:15 AM: Regret waking up. 6:30 AM: Study. 6:45 AM: Stare at the wall and contemplate the meaning of cube roots. It was all there

— color—coded, laminated (in my imagination), and blessed by three highlighters.

My mother, meanwhile, had already drawn up a strategic career blueprint. She called it "Operation Future Teacher." It had arrows, timelines, and motivational quotes like *"Teaching is the one profession that creates all other professions"* — which she repeated every time I tried to sneak in a nap.

She believed in me. Fiercely. Like a coach cheering from the sidelines while I tried to wrestle with prime factorization and the laws of motion. Her dream was clear: I'd become a teacher. I'd wear crisp sarees, carry red pens, and say things like *"Class, settle down"* with majestic authority.

And me? I was determined. I wasn't aiming for perfection — just progress. Seventy percent was my golden ticket. The first step toward chalkboards, lesson plans, and maybe one day, inspiring a student the way my teachers inspired me.

Sure, the journey had potholes — sleepy mornings, confusing formulas, and the occasional existential crisis over cube roots — but I was on my way. One timetable block at a time.

The first exam was over and with the sigh of relief, I relaxed, having put in that extra bit of effort. Now I was poised and ready for the next set of chapters, as we embarked on the summative exam. I had full confidence that my plans are perfectly aligned with my goals. But, as fate would have it, destiny had other plans in store.

It was a perfectly ordinary day. The sun was shining. My pen was working. My hair was behaving. The teacher called out, “Pass down the corrected books.” I nodded like a responsible citizen of the classroom republic, turned around to hand them to the back row, and — BAM! I was hit with the most adorable, loving stare. The gentle admiration in his gaze wrapped around my heart, filling me with sense of wonder. Only then, memories came flooding back. “I had seen those eyes even before. I had felt exactly the same way even before. When was it? OMG! He’s the same boy from the spelling bee competition. I hadn’t recognized him for months now.

The spark of recognition ignited a fire storm of emotions within me. Being caught in a glance was making me nervous and flustered. I was torn between being impressed and feeling embarrassed. I didn't understand how to process these thoughts and out of nowhere a bolt of thunder and lightning struck me with electrifying force, as if the very heavens had conspired to jolt me out of my wits. The shockwave coursed through my entire being, leaving me shaken, bewildered and wide—eyed with wonder. And then, like a specter haunting my every waking thought, a single thrilling question echoed through my mind "How on earth would I sit next to him as my bench partner?"

It wasn't just a question. It was a challenge. A cosmic dare. A romantic horror—comedy waiting to happen.

I imagined it – sitting beside him, sharing desk space, possibly exchanging pens, and maybe even... accidentally brushing elbows. My soul screamed. My timetable wept. My inner introvert packed a suitcase and considered moving to the library permanently.

Would I be able to focus? Would I forget how to spell my own name? Would I start quoting Newton's laws just to sound smart?

And yet... beneath the panic, there was a strange thrill. A spark. A whisper of possibility. Maybe this wasn't just fate playing tricks. Maybe it was fate offering a new storyline – one with awkward glances, shared textbooks, and the kind of bench partnership that could rewrite my entire school chapter.

I didn’t know what would happen next. But I knew one thing for sure:

This was no longer just about seventy percent. This was about surviving the emotional rollercoaster of sitting next to the boy who once spelled “benevolent” and now looked at me like I was the plot twist he didn’t see coming.

I took a deep breath, squared my shoulders and told myself to get a grip. I couldn't let my nerves get the better of me. I had to find a way to compose myself, to be confident and to show him that I was more than just a nervous wreck. And so, I came up with the most straight forward solution ‘ignorance’. I would pretend to know nothing.

Yes. I would pretend to know *nothing*. Not his name. Not his spelling bee glory. Not the fact that his stare had short–circuited my brain like a rogue lightning bolt.

If he said “Hi,” I’d blink politely.

If he asked for a pen, I’d hand it over like a bored librarian.

If he solved a math problem in 0.3 seconds, I'd nod like I hadn't just witnessed academic sorcery.

I was going to be chill. Ice—cold chill. The kind of chill that says, *"I don't even know you're the topper. I just sit here because the teacher said so."*

Of course, inside, my thoughts were doing backflips. My emotions were hosting a circus. And my heart was composing poetry in his honor.

But on the outside? I was the queen of casual. The empress of "Oh, you're here too?" The silent storm beneath the surface.

I became an expert at avoiding eye contact, staring intently at the clock, the blackboard or even the floor. Anything to avoid meeting his gaze. But the distraction was shot lived, and my thoughts inevitably drifted back to him as if he was my final destination which I cannot escape.

The game of 'I don't see you' went on for days, yet in this silence we both heard the unspoken truth only strengthening the illusionary connection between us. I discovered a beautiful symmetry in our interest and values, harmony that resonated deep within us.

It was as if our bond was always meant to be, a union of two souls who found a sense of home in each other. I thought I was calm – the one who could handle surprise tests and tangled emotions with grace. But he was the calmest. Like a still lake that reflected everything without a ripple. I considered myself kind – the kind who offered extra paper and smiled at lost pencils. But he was the kindest. Quietly generous, effortlessly gentle, like kindness was woven into his DNA.

He was always five steps ahead. Not just in academics, but in presence. He knew when to speak and when silence said more. He solved problems before I even found the question. And somehow, without words, he made me feel seen.

We never exchanged jokes. Never shared secrets. But every time our eyes met, it felt like a conversation – one that didn't need sound. A bond not built on chatter, but on quiet understanding. Like two stars orbiting the same sky, aware of each other's glow.

The only conversations between us were *explanations*. Not "Hi," not "How was your day?" – Just pure, academic, syllabus–approved *explanations*. And yet, somehow, they felt like secret messages wrapped in algebra.

He'd lean slightly forward, notebook in hand, and say,
"Can you explain this part again?"
And I'd blink, suspicious. *"Teasing me!"* I'd think. *"The topper of the class asking me?"*
But then I'd see it — that sweet, little smile. The one with the crinkling eyes. The one that said more than words ever could:

"I want to see you a little more. I want to hear you a little more."

It wasn't about formulas anymore. It wasn't about cube roots or prime factorization. It was about the quiet rhythm we shared — the way he listened, the way I explained, the way our silences filled the space between sentences.

It was a delicate balance. Intellect and emotion, logic and longing. A classroom connection that tiptoed between chalk, dust and heartbeats.

And in those moments, the explanation became secondary.

It was the *connection* that mattered.
The way he looked at me like I was the answer to a question he hadn't dared to ask.

That day, our science teacher was absent, and the classroom transformed into a little universe of its own. The chatter of gossiping kids filled the air like birds fluttering in spring—light, loud, and everywhere. Scholars huddled in corners, deep in discussion, their voices weaving theories and equations like threads in a tapestry. But I? I found my sanctuary beside him. Exactly where I meant to be, where I belong.

While the world spun in its own rhythm, I sat next to him like a devotee beside a saint—quiet, content, and completely absorbed in the serenity of his presence. No words passed between us, no glances exchanged, yet the silence felt sacred. It was the kind of moment that didn't need decoration. Just being there, beside him, was enough.

I would spend my entire life beside him like this, happily. His mere existence was enough to excite me. His presence was my peace, my chaos, my everything.

He was immersed in his science problems, pencil dancing across the page. I, pretending to scribble in my notebook, was secretly sketching the contours of this moment into memory.

Then came the interruption — our side benchers, loud and curious, diving headfirst into a conversation that had nothing to do with science and everything to do with scandalous fun. One of them had apparently watched a late—night TV show about palmistry and was now the self—declared guru of love lines and fate.

"Show me your hand!" one of them demanded, grabbing another's palm like a detective examining clues. "See this line? That's your love line. And it's broken — heartbreak alert!"

The group erupted into gasps and giggles, as if someone had just predicted a Bollywood—style breakup. Another chimed in, "If your lifeline and heart line join, it means love marriage is written in your destiny!"

Suddenly, the classroom wasn't a classroom anymore — it was a chaotic mix of a fortune—teller's tent and a reality show. Palms were flying in the air, fingers tracing imaginary futures, and dramatic declarations like “You’ll marry twice!” or “You’ll fall in love with your best friend!” echoed off the walls.

I tried to stay focused, but the energy was infectious. Even he looked up from his notebook, amused. I barely registered their words until he suddenly turned to me, palms joined, lifelines aligned, and held them up close to my face.

“Joining lifelines shows possibility of love marriage,” he said, eyes twinkling with mischief.

I blinked, startled, and then lifted both my palms to mimic the gesture. But before I could align them, he reached out, took my left hand gently, and pressed it to his right palm.

“Ooh, they are joining!” he declared with a grin, laughter bubbling from his lips.

I stared at our hands, confused and flustered, heart thudding like a drum. “Isn’t it my both palms that need to be joined... not yours?” I asked, half–serious, half–lost in the moment.

He laughed even harder, the kind of laugh that makes the world feel lighter. "But this is more fun," he said, eyes dancing. His voice teasing, but his eyes... his eyes were something else entirely. They sparkled, yes — but not just with mischief. There was softness there, a flicker of something tender, like he was letting me peek into a dream he'd been carrying quietly for a long time.

As if, in that silly moment of joined palms and playful fate, he was trying to tell me something he couldn't say out loud.
As if he was showing me the version of us he imagined — not just in that classroom, but in a thousand quiet futures.

And just like that, the classroom faded. The gossip, the equations, the noise — all dissolved into the background. All that remained was the warmth of his hand, the echo of his laughter, and the innocent thrill of a moment that felt like a secret shared with the universe.

Life was unfolding like a soft melody, each day humming its own tune, each moment carrying a quiet kind of beauty. It was our final year of school — a time when everything felt fleeting yet full of promise. The air was thick with last chances and lingering glances, and every gathering felt like a memory in the making.

One afternoon, my best friend and I were invited to a birthday party — a celebration hosted by one of our newer classmates. The kind of invite that felt casual on the surface but held the weight of something special. He was on the guest list too. The boy who made silence feel sacred. The one whose presence could turn an ordinary day into something worth remembering.

I was hopeful. Hopeful for laughter, for shared cake and silly game. Hopeful that this party, this simple celebration, would become one of those memories we'd carry with us long after the school bell rang for the last time.

It was supposed to be carefree — a burst of joy in the middle of our slow goodbye.

But little did I know, the evening was about to turn grey and black — not in the sky, but in the undercurrent of something I couldn't yet name. What began as a simple birthday celebration, a night meant for laughter and memories, slowly began to shift in hue.

My best friend had brought her cousin along – a last–minute addition, she said, just someone to tag along so she wouldn't feel awkward arriving with only me. She introduced us casually, and I offered a polite yet detached "hello." My tone was neutral, my smile thin. I didn't think much of it. Just another face in the crowd, another name I wouldn't remember.

But that brief, seemingly insignificant exchange would mark the beginning of something I never saw coming.

We stepped inside the party, arms full of gifts and good intentions. The room was warm with music and chatter, fairy lights blinking like stars strung across the ceiling. Her cousin, meanwhile, claimed he had a friend to meet nearby and slipped away with a wave and a smile.

Or so we thought.

What we didn't know – what we couldn't have imagined – was that he never really left. While we laughed and danced and posed for photos, he lingered outside. Not just passing time. Hovering in the shadows like a question mark at the end of a sentence we hadn't written yet.

And though the night carried on with cake and candles, something in the air had shifted. A thread had been pulled. And soon, everything would begin to unravel.

Despite the festive atmosphere, I couldn't shake off the feeling of unease. The knowledge that he was lingering outside, watching and waiting made my skin crawl. I had a bad feeling about his intentions and I couldn't help but think he was trying to hit on me. The thought alone made me uncomfortable and I desperately wanted to avoid any further encounter with him.

As the party came to an end, we waved everyone goodbye — smiles exchanged, promises of staying in touch, the usual echoes of a night well spent. My best friend and I stepped out into the cool evening, walking along the familiar road that had always felt safe, ordinary.

But tonight, something felt off.

My discomfort, subtle at first, began to sharpen with each step. A strange heaviness settled in my chest, like a warning whispered by instinct. And then, like a scene unfolding exactly as feared, he appeared.

Her cousin.

He emerged from the shadows with a casual air, as if bumping into us was pure coincidence. But I knew better. His timing was too perfect, his presence too deliberate. He tried to engage me in conversation — light words, harmless questions — but I remained silent, my gaze fixed ahead, my steps quickening.

He didn't take the hint.

His behavior once brushed off as awkward or overly friendly, began to unravel into something more unsettling. There was a pattern to it — the way he lingered, the way he watched, the way he spoke as if we shared a secret I didn't know I was keeping. It wasn't just persistence. It was a psyche. A quiet, calculated presence that made my skin crawl.

And as the streetlights flickered above us, I realized this wasn't just a strange encounter. It was the beginning of something I hadn't prepared for — a shift in the story I thought I was writing.

He looked me in the eye and said, with blunt force: *"If you had any relationship with a boy other than me, I would kill that boy."* No hesitation. No humor. Just a threat — raw, possessive, and terrifying.

My heart froze. My mind raced. Was this a joke? A twisted attempt at attention? But his face was calm. Too calm. And that's when it hit me: this wasn't affection. This was control. This was obsession disguised as interest. This was dangerous.

I didn't respond. I couldn't. My instincts screamed to get away, to protect my space, to shield my peace. And I did. I walked away. I chose silence over confrontation, distance over drama.

But inside, I was shaken. Bewildered. Angry.

Because no one — *no one* — has the right to speak to me like that. To claim ownership over my choices. To threaten violence in the name of attention.

That moment taught me something powerful: My boundaries are sacred. My safety is non—negotiable. And my silence, in that moment, was not weakness — it was wisdom.

As I learned more about him, my unease began to shift — slow and steady — into something sharper. Fear.

He was a boxing champion at his school, a title that should've inspired admiration. But the gleam of his medals couldn't hide the shadows that trailed behind him. Whispers floated through the corridors — rumors of minor altercations, sudden bursts of temper, confrontations that never made it to the principal's office but lived vividly in the stories students told.

His behavior toward me had already raised red flags. The way he lingered too long, the way his gaze felt more like a challenge than curiosity. There was something in his presence that felt off — like a storm disguised as calm.

He didn't seem like a misunderstood boy. He seemed like a dangerous villain in a story I hadn't agreed to be part of.

The more I thought about it, the more the pieces began to fit — and the picture they formed was unsettling. That night, I lay awake, the ceiling above me fading into darkness as my mind raced with worries.

What did he want?

Why me?

Was I just imagining it – or was something truly wrong?

The silence of the night offered no answers. Only the echo of my own heartbeat, loud and uncertain.

I decided to brush it off and not let it bother me. Maybe he was just talking big–trying to stir something up without any real intention behind it. I told myself not to overthink, not to let his words take root in my mind. So I tried to relax, to carry on with my day as if nothing had changed. I packed my bag, stepped out into the morning air, and headed to school like it was just another ordinary day.

But beneath the surface, I was more alert than usual. My eyes scanned the corridors with quiet caution, my steps slightly quicker, my voice a little more reserved. I distanced myself from the person who made my heart feel safe, simply because the shadows cast by another had begun to blur my clarity – not because I didn't want to see him, but because I didn't want to risk drawing attention. I didn't want to create unnecessary tension or give anyone a reason to twist things further.

It hurt, in a quiet way. That kind of ache that doesn't shout, but lingers. I missed the comfort of his presence, the way his smile could soften the edges of a hard day. But for now, distance felt safer. I hoped he'd understand, even if I couldn't explain. I just prayed, this storm would pass without ever breaking.

Days passed and I thought the incident was behind me. But what I didn't know was that, something even more unsettling was waiting to happen. As my best friend and I were walking home from school, engrossed in gossip, a bold, curdling scream pierced through the air. My heart sank as I heard my name being shouted followed by confession of love. I turned to see the psychopath standing atop a hill behind the school. His voice echoing through the valley like a man possessed. That moment left me traumatized and I am still haunted by that memory.

I now knew — the water had risen above my head. Not just metaphorically, but emotionally, spiritually. I was drowning in a sea of fear, and every breath felt like a borrowed moment. My lungs ached, not from exertion, but from the weight of everything I couldn't say aloud.

Each thought was a frantic paddle toward safety. Each heartbeat a silent scream. But the more I struggled, the more the current pulled me under. I was trapped – not in a room, not in a situation, but in a *nightmare.* A waking dream with no exit sign, no lifeline, no voice to call my own.

The fear was not loud. It was quiet. Crippling. Like invisible vines wrapping around my chest, squeezing tighter with every passing day. I looked around, hoping someone would notice – a glance, a gesture, a question. But silence met silence. And I stayed quiet too, unsure if my truth would be understood or dismissed.

All I could do was feel. Feel the crushing weight of my predicament. Feel the ache of isolation. Feel the haunting echo of that scream on the hill, still ringing in my ears like a curse I never asked for.

But even in that darkness, something flickered. A whisper. A spark. A truth:

I am still here.
I am still breathing.
And even if the world doesn't see it yet – I am fighting.

My best friend and I sprinted home desperate to escape him. She was shaken too, having never expected the psychopath to cross the line like that. Now, as soon as I reached home I couldn't stop thinking about how to deal with him and most pressingly, how I would face tomorrow, knowing I had to walk to school on the same rout again.

The next day, I walked to school with the sense of dread. I was terrified that the psychopath might be lurking around the corner, waiting to pounce on me with another unwanted confession. I was getting ready for the worst–case scenario. I found myself silently praying that I wouldn't run into him. As I approach the school gate, I got a sight of the psychopath standing at the distance. It seemed like we had just missed each other by a matter of minute. I breathed a sigh of relief, grateful that I had dodged the bullet and avoided another uncomfortable encounter.

Just as I was trying to navigate the awkwardness with the psychopath, the boy I actually had feelings for was finally finding the courage to reveal his true feelings to me.

On that particular day, he approached me with a casual ease, like it was just another conversation between friends. I didn't expect anything unusual. I was too busy trying to keep my emotional balance, too focused on not letting the chaos around me seep into the spaces that mattered. But then out of the blue, he uttered the secret—spell that would forever change the course of our friendship. His voice trembled with conviction, his sincerity echoed deep within my soul as he said "I love you".

It wasn't dramatic. It wasn't rehearsed. It was real. And in that instant, the air around us shifted. The world didn't explode, but something inside me did—a quiet bloom of warmth, surprise, and something dangerously close to joy.

I was caught off guard. Unsure of how to react, I froze, pretending I hadn't heard him. I kept my head down, avoiding eye contact, and continued scribbling in my notebook, trying to ply it cool. But within I was torn between my growing concern and genuine feelings. I stood at a crossroads, uncertain how to navigate my emotions while protecting him and myself from the clutches of psychopath.

The silence hung between us like a fragile thread, stretched taut by everything unsaid. He stood there for a moment, eyes flickering with vulnerability, and then turned away—his shoulders slightly hunched, and his steps uneven with emotion. I watched him walk out of the class, and though the room was full of noise and movement, all I could see was him.

My gaze clung to his retreating figure, caught in a storm of concern and compassion. I wanted to reach out, to say something that would soften the blow, but the words refused to come. My heart ached with guilt—for not reciprocating, for letting him walk away with his feelings exposed and unanswered. But my mind screamed caution. It reminded me of the chaos I was already entangled in, the risks of letting emotions lead when the ground beneath me was anything but stable.

I sat there, frozen in that moment, torn between the warmth of what could be and the cold logic of what must be. And somewhere deep inside, I wondered if he'd ever understand that my silence wasn't rejection—it was protection. For both of us.

For the first time, I realized how delicate and fragile our emotions can be—how they flutter just beneath the surface, unseen yet powerful, like the wings of a butterfly caught in a storm. One moment, everything feels steady, familiar, safe. And then, with a single word, a glance, or a silence too long, the balance shifts.

Emotions aren't loud. They don't always announce themselves. Sometimes they whisper in the quiet corners of our hearts, tugging gently, asking to be heard. Other times, they surge like waves, overwhelming and raw. But always, they are tender—easily bruised, easily misunderstood.

I saw it in his eyes as he walked away, in the way my own heart twisted with guilt and caution. I felt it in the silence that followed, heavy with things left unsaid. And I understood, in that moment, that feelings aren't just fleeting impulses. They're fragile truths we carry, hoping someone else will hold them with care.

The stories which I once used to hear from my friends about love or watch a rom—com on screen, dismissing them with a careless laugh, rolling my eyes at sappy—cheesy scenes on TV with a scoff. Love, sincerity and vulnerability now weighted heavily upon me. The difference was, I was no longer just hearing about them in stories from friends, I was living them, feeling their tender touch and their crushing weight.

As I struggled with the consequences of my unspoken emotions, he mistook my silence for rejection. I watched him retreat—not with anger, but with a quiet ache, slipping into the shadows of his own vulnerability. It wasn't the kind of departure that slammed doors or raised voices. It was softer, sadder. Like a song that fades before the final note.

My affectionate smile had whispered promises I wasn't brave enough to speak aloud. It had hinted at warmth, at something tender blooming beneath the surface. But my silence—my silence had shouted rejection. It had drowned out every subtle gesture, every glance that might have said "wait, there's more."

I couldn't help but wonder if he felt cheated. Cheated by the way I oscillated between closeness and caution, between the pull of affection and the push of fear. Did he feel like I'd offered him a glimpse of something beautiful, only to snatch it away before he could hold it?

Between us, a heavy mist of grief began to settle. It didn't divide us with anger—it blurred the lines, softened the edges, and turned everything into shades of grey. Not love, not loss. Just the quiet ache of what could have been.

From that day on, he began to distance himself from me—not with words, but with absence. The way he stopped looking my way, the way his laughter no longer reached me. It wasn't sudden. It was gradual, like dusk swallowing daylight.

As he turned away, I felt a sting of regret—a sharp, bitter taste of what could have been. A future that had flickered for a moment, and then vanished before it could take shape. I hadn't meant to hurt him, but silence has its own language, and mine had spoken too loudly.

His avoidance and neglect weren't loud either. But they were piercing. They made me feel humiliated, disrespected, and broken. Like a slow—burning fire that didn't rage, didn't roar—but smoldered quietly, consuming me bit by bit. Each day, I woke up hoping for a shift, a glance, a word. And each day, I was met with the same cold distance.

I began to question myself. Was I cruel for not responding? Was I selfish for protecting my own heart?

Or was I simply human—caught between fear and feeling, between caution and longing?

The silence had become our new language—an unspoken agreement carved from hesitation and hurt. It filled the spaces between us, thick and suffocating, until even the simplest words felt foreign. We stood as strangers now, not because we had forgotten each other, but because we remembered too much.

Emotions once warm and fluid had hardened into ice. They no longer flowed freely; they cracked and splintered beneath the weight of everything we didn't say. Our hearts, once open and curious, now wore armor forged from misunderstanding and fear.

Our eyes, once bright with connection—those glances that used to carry laughter, secrets, and silent comfort—now darted away like guilty confessions. As if the mere act of meeting each other's gaze had become unbearable. As if looking too long might unravel the fragile distance we'd built to protect ourselves.

And yet, beneath all that cold, something still flickered. A memory. A longing. A quiet ache that whispered, *we were more than this*. But neither of us dared to reach through the frost.

Final exam loomed. I made a conscious decision to set aside my emotional hazard, to temporarily shelve the ache in my heart, and prioritize my academic pursuits. I sought refuge in my studies, using the discipline and structure to keep my mind occupied and my emotions at bay.

Not much sooner, the day of our final school year arrived—a bittersweet milestone that marked the end of an era. The corridors echoed with laughter, nostalgia, and the rustle of farewell notes passed between friends. Everyone wore smiles tinged with sadness, trying to freeze fleeting moments before they dissolved into memory.

As all the classmates gathered to bid farewell, I felt the weight of time pressing gently on my shoulders. And then, through the crowd, I saw him. whose presence had once stirred both comfort and confusion.

He didn't say much. He didn't need to. He simply offered me a gentle smile—a quiet acknowledgment that this was our final goodbye. It didn't echo. It didn't sting. It simply...faded. Like the last note of a lullaby, lingering in the silence it left behind. With the grace of letting go.

In that moment, I understood that some stories don't end with closure. They end with a glance, a smile, and the silent promise that even if we drift apart, we once mattered.

We were walking across the playground, the air light with shared silence, when suddenly—like a gust of interruption—a girl from our class appeared between us. She didn't hesitate. With a boldness that caught both of us off guard, she turned to him and asked, "How do I look? Am I looking good or not?"

He froze. His expression flickered with panic, and then—shattered by the pressure—he blurted out, "You look good."

The words hung awkwardly in the air, brittle and misplaced. I felt the moment fracture. Not wanting to make it worse, I quietly stepped away, giving them space. But before I could disappear into the crowd, I heard my name—his voice trailing behind me like a thread refusing to break.

I turned around. He stood there, guilt written all over him, like a boy who'd knocked over something precious and didn't know how to fix it. I tilted my head, silently asking, "What?"

"I'm sorry," he said, eyes flickering with guilt. "You look way better than her."

Even today, those words bring a smile to my face—not because of the compliment, but because of the way he said it. Awkward, sincere, and just a little panicked, as if he was trying to patch a wound with words that barely held together. It wasn't perfect, but it was real.

He tried to hide his guilt behind a half–smile and a flurry of movement, diving into the task at hand with exaggerated focus. As he worked on the alterations—hands steady, brows furrowed in concentration—he appeared to be irresistibly cute. Every stitch, every adjustment felt like a quiet apology, woven into fabric instead of spoken aloud.

His meticulous movements said what his words couldn't: *I care. I messed up. I'm trying.* And somehow, that mattered more than any grand gesture.

With this, I closed the first ever chapter of my life—an unfinished tale, delicate and incomplete, like the fading scent of autumn leaves. It didn't end with resolution, but with quiet echoes and soft regrets. The pages weren't torn, just left open, fluttering gently in the wind of memory.

Some moments remained unwritten, some emotions unspoken. But perhaps that's how first chapters are meant to be—not perfect, not polished, but raw and real. A mosaic of laughter, heartbreak, silence, and longing.

And as I walked away from that playground, from that final smile, I carried the weight of what was and the wonder of what might have been. The scent of autumn lingered—not in the air, but in my heart.

Growing up, I wore the label "good girl" like a crown. I sat straight, spoke softly, and followed every rule with religious fervor. Teachers adored me. Parents pointed to me as the gold standard. I didn't just behave—I performed goodness. And I loved it.

But with that halo came a shadow.

I began to see the "bad kids" not as children, but as cautionary tales. The ones who got demoted, who talked back, who colored outside the lines—I judged them with the quiet cruelty of someone who believed she'd earned moral superiority. I didn't just follow the rules; I became their enforcer. I was the self-appointed guardian of virtue, silently condemning anyone who strayed.

And then came the twist.

My rigid morality, my obsession with being good, made me blind. Blind to nuance. Blind to danger. I ignored red flags because they didn't fit my script. I trusted people who praised my goodness, even when their smiles didn't reach their eyes. I dismissed warnings from "bad kids" because, well, what did they know?

That's how I ended up being chased by a psychopath. The irony? My judgmental pride—my belief that goodness was armor—left me exposed. Vulnerable. The very kids I once looked down on would've spotted the danger. They'd lived in chaos. They knew how to read it. But I was too busy being good to notice I was walking into a nightmare.

4. Psychopath: From fear to survival.

After our board exam results were announced, I was thrilled to have secured a first – class grade. I felt like I had successfully crossed the first hurdle. Completing this level was a huge accomplishment and now I was ready to move on to the next challenge: the second level of Higher Secondary Education.

My best friend was devastated. Second class. The words hit her like a betrayal wrapped in exam sheets. She stared at her marks as if they'd personally insulted her ancestors. And then she turned to me—First class, glowing like a smug little sun—and her expression shifted from shock to theatrical outrage.

We had studied together during the holidays. Shared notes, snacks, and sleepless nights. So how *dare* I outscore her? She looked at me as if I'd secretly bribed the examiner or hacked the grading system. Honestly, I felt like handing her a gold medal in tantrums—Category: "Best Performance in Academic Meltdown."

She was so mad at me for being smarter than her. As if I had set the question paper myself, tailored it to my strengths, and left her to fend for herself in a jungle of algebra and history dates.

I tried to console her, but she was busy rehearsing her villain origin story. And yet, beneath all the drama, I knew she'd bounce back. Because that's what best friends do—they throw tantrums, they sulk, and then they laugh with you again. Eventually.

Now came the time to choose a college—a decision that should have felt like a celebration, a step toward dreams. But for me, it was tangled in fear and hesitation.

Admission to my dream college was within reach. I had earned the marks, and it was the same place where I had completed my schooling. Familiar walls, familiar faces. Yet, familiarity wasn't comfort anymore—it was a reminder of danger.

The psychopath who had stalked me during school had often waited outside the gates, his presence like a shadow that refused to fade. The thought of returning there, without the shield of my friends—most of who were planning to attend a different college—made my heart sink.

My mother suggested I enroll there. She saw the convenience, the continuity. But I saw the risk. I was afraid of being alone. Afraid that without my friends, I'd be vulnerable again. That he'd find me, watch me, corner me.

And so, I stood at a crossroads—between ambition and safety, between the familiar and the secure. I knew this choice wasn't just about academics. It was about reclaiming my life, protecting my peace, and choosing a future where I could breathe freely.

After careful consideration, I chose to prioritize my safety. The world felt uncertain, and I knew I couldn't afford to walk into the unknown alone. So I enrolled in the college where my friends would be studying—not just for academics, but for the comfort of familiar faces, for the quiet reassurance of trust.

It wasn't a decision born of fear, but of wisdom. I wanted to be surrounded by people who knew me, who could read the silence between my words, who would stand beside me if shadows ever returned. In their presence, I felt less like a target and more like a person reclaiming her peace.

Sometimes, choosing safety means choosing connection. And in that moment, I chose both.

The initial days of college were filled with joy and new experiences. Everything felt fresh—new faces, new routines, and a sense of freedom I hadn't tasted in a long time. I laughed more, breathed easier, and for a while, I allowed myself to believe that the past had finally loosened its grip on me.

I had momentarily forgotten about the psychopath. The distance between his house and the college felt like a protective barrier, a stretch of safety that I clung to with quiet hope. Surely, he wouldn't chase me this far. Surely, he'd let go.

But my relief was short—lived.

It began with a flicker—a familiar name whispered in passing, a glance that lingered too long, a chill that crept down my spine without warning. The shadows I thought I'd outrun began to stretch again, reaching into the corners of my new life. And just like that, the illusion of safety cracked.

I realized then: distance doesn't always mean escape. Some threats don't respect boundaries. Some stories refuse to stay buried.

To my horror, the stalking began again.

This time, it wasn't subtle. He climbed onto the terrace of the building adjacent to mine—an eerie perch from which he could watch me, wave at me, and call out my name like it was some twisted game. From that vantage point, he turned my home into a stage, and I was the unwilling performer under his gaze.

What terrified me most wasn't just his presence—it was his audacity. He seemed to have no fear of my parents, no shame, and no hesitation. His actions weren't just invasive; they were defiant. As if boundaries didn't apply to him. As if my discomfort was irrelevant.

I felt trapped. My own home, once a place of comfort, now felt like a cage with glass walls. Every movement felt exposed. Every moment of peace was interrupted by the looming question: *What is he capable of next?*

The fear wasn't loud—it was quiet and constant. Like a shadow that followed me from room to room. And in that silence, I realized how deeply harassment can seep into your life—not just through actions, but through the loss of safety, the erosion of trust, and the haunting uncertainty of what comes next.

Now that he was trespassing into my personal space, the fear became tangible. He began to frequent the area around my house—lingering near the gates, pacing the street, appearing at odd hours with a gaze that felt invasive and deliberate. It wasn't just proximity anymore. It was possession. A silent claim over the spaces I once considered safe.

There was something in his eyes—something cold, calculating, and disturbingly amused. I sensed a malicious intent behind his gaze. And slowly, I did. I began to question myself, to shrink within my own skin. The feeling wasn't just fear—it was self—loathing. As if I had somehow invited this, failed to stop it, failed to protect myself.

I avoided windows. I flinched at footsteps. I stopped smiling in my own home. His presence didn't just haunt the streets—it haunted my thoughts. And in that haunting, I felt myself fading.

I had spent my entire 10th standard trying to ignore him, hoping he'd lose interest and move on. But I was wrong. He refuse to surrender, and he's obsession only grew stronger with each passing day.

As the months dragged on, his fixation became a living nightmare. I struggled to sleep as I kept turning and tossing all night trying to find a way out of this situation. The pressure was mounting from every direction, like the walls of crushing vice, squeezing the life out of me.

I refused to go to the market alone. I avoided the streets I once walked freely, the corners of my neighborhood that used to feel familiar. Every outing became a calculated risk, every shadow a potential threat. The fear of crossing paths with him had seeped into my daily life, shrinking my world into a cage of caution.

But I couldn't live like this forever.

His relentless pursuit had taken a toll—not just on my safety, but on my spirit. My social health began to crumble. I stopped meeting friends, stopped laughing freely, and stopped being myself. I was surviving, not living.

And that's when something shifted.

I realized that fear, left unchecked, becomes a prison. So I decided to take a stand. No more shrinking. No more silence. I raised my guards—not just emotionally, but practically. I began to prepare, not just to defend, but to reclaim. To counter his presence with strength, with strategy, with support.

Because if he was planning his next move, I would be ready. And this time, I wouldn't be the one running.

It was time to take a stand, raise my guards, and prepare a counter attack before he could strike.

At first, I thought of telling my mother. I wanted to speak the truth—to let her know about his harassing actions, the threats, and the fear that had begun to shape my every step. But something held me back.

It wasn't silence born of shame. It was uncertainty. I wasn't sure how she would react. Would she protect me? Or would she panic and send me away to my uncle's place, far from everything I knew? The thought of being uprooted, of losing my routine, my friends, and my fragile sense of normalcy—it scared me almost as much as he did.

I didn't want to be treated like a problem to be relocated. I wanted to be heard. I wanted someone to stand beside me, not just shield me from afar. But in that moment, I couldn't predict whether my truth would bring comfort or consequence.

So I stayed quiet. For a little longer. Watching. Waiting. Hoping for the right moment to speak—and for the strength to be believed.

I had already spent my childhood at my aunt's place. My life had been one of constant movement—a banjara soul, never rooted, always shifting. Born in one place, raised in another, passed between the care of my uncle and then sent away again to study at my aunt's house. I had learned to pack my emotions lightly, to carry memories like folded letters in a suitcase that never stayed shut for long.

But now... now I was finally home.

Living with my parents and siblings, I had begun to taste what it meant to belong—not just to a place, but to a family. To wake up to familiar voices, to share meals, to argue over little things and laugh over nothing. It wasn't perfect, but it was mine. And I didn't want to lose it.

The thought of being sent away again—of being uprooted because of someone else's cruelty—filled me with dread. I had just begun to feel grounded, and I wasn't ready to let that go. Not again.

My life had taken me through a scorching desert, battered by torrential rains. I was parched for peace, desperately seeking refuge in a tranquil oasis—somewhere I could breathe without flinching, exist without fear.

I thought the first chapter of my life was closed. Sealed. Forgotten. But it wasn't. It had simply turned a page, and now it followed me into college.

He was there. Perhaps in the same college. Perhaps in the same class. His presence was surreal—like a ghost that didn't haunt, but numbed. He didn't storm into my life this time. He drifted in, quiet and calculated. And strangely, his presence calmed my nerves. Like a tranquilizer. Not because I trusted him, but because I knew where the danger was. And when you've lived in chaos long enough, even the familiar threat feels safer than the unknown.

He tried to reach out. To reconnect. To rewrite the narrative. But I was resolute. I shut him down with silence, with distance, with a smile that masked the thousand shattered pieces beneath.

I wore that smile like armor. Polished, practiced, convincing. But inside, I was still gathering the fragments of myself—still learning how to be whole in a world that had once broken me.

But more than him, my mind was consumed by thoughts of the psychopath.

His presence lingered like smoke—unseen but suffocating. Even when he wasn't near, I felt him watching, waiting, and calculating. I couldn't focus on classes, couldn't enjoy the company of others. My thoughts spiraled around one question: *How do I cut him out of my life permanently?*

It wasn't just fear anymore. It was exhaustion. I was tired of flinching at shadows, tired of second—guessing every step, tired of feeling like a prisoner in my own story. I wanted peace—not borrowed, not temporary, but lasting.

I began to think in strategies. Not just escape, but defense. Not just silence, but action. I knew I couldn't live like this forever. Something had to change. I had to change.

Because survival wasn't enough anymore. I wanted freedom.

One fine day, a boy from my class approached me—eyes red, voice trembling, and tears threatening to spill. I braced myself for something serious, something tragic. But what he said next made my blood run cold... and my jaw drop in disbelief.

He asked me, with genuine concern, *"Are you really his girlfriend?"*

I blinked. "*Whose?*"
"The psychopath's brother", he clarified.
Apparently, the brother had told my classmate that I was his girlfriend—studying in the same college, just in a different field. As if we were some secret couple living parallel lives.

I stared at him in horror. Not because of the question, but because of what it revealed. This wasn't just one disturbed individual. It was an entire family tangled in delusion. A web of mental instability that seemed to stretch far beyond what I had imagined.

The boy was shedding tears—not for me, but for the sheer absurdity of the situation. And honestly, I felt like handing him a tissue and a reality check. Because this wasn't just bizarre—it was dangerous.

I realized then that I wasn't just dealing with a stalker. I was dealing with a family narrative that had rewritten my identity without my consent. And that was terrifying.

My blood started boiling.

The absurdity of the situation, the false claims, and the twisted narratives—it all surged through me like fire. And just then, my crush, who had been quietly observing from behind, leaned in with a suggestion that made me scoff.

"You should get a boyfriend," he said, half—serious, half—hopeful.
I didn't need to decode the subtext. He meant himself.

I rolled my eyes. Not now. Not this. I wasn't looking for romance—I was looking for refuge.

Ignoring him, I marched straight to the psychopath's brother. I needed answers. I needed to confront the lies, the delusions, and the bizarre claim that I was his girlfriend. But as I marched to meet up with the brother, something shifted in me.

I found myself circling back to the suggestion—*get a boyfriend.* Not for love. Not for companionship. But for protection.

By now, I had no doubt. The stalker was a real psychopath. He would come after me sooner or later. He would confess his twisted version of love, and I would reject him—firmly, clearly, without hesitation.

But then what?

Would he quietly accept it? Absolutely not. He hadn't stopped in the past year, despite my countless attempts to reject, ignore, and distance myself. He kept coming. Kept watching. Kept invading.

And now, the stakes were higher.

What if he tried to harm me? What if he hurt someone I cared about? He was a boxer champion—strong, short-tempered, and above all, mentally unstable. The thought of his rage, his unpredictability, ran through every drop of my blood like a warning bell.

I needed a shield. Someone he wouldn't dare to cross. Someone who could stand between me and the storm.

And ironically, the only person who fit that role... was his own brother.

It wasn't love. It wasn't desire. It was survival. A calculated move to protect myself from a threat that refused to fade. If aligning with his brother could keep me safe—could stop the harassment, the stalking, the fear—then maybe, just maybe, it was worth considering. Sometimes, the heart doesn't choose. The mind does. And mine was screaming for safety.

I got goose bumps at the very thought.

It wasn't just a strategy—it was a sacrifice. My conscience whispered, almost pleading: *Are you prepared to trade your integrity for survival?* The question echoed through me like thunder in a hollow cave.

I stood at the edge of a moral cliff, juggling between self—preservation and self—respect. Could I really drop my values, wear the mask of love, and hide behind it like a shield against the psychopath? Could I gamble with something as sacred as my truth just to stay safe?

The mist of confusion swirled around me, thick and suffocating. But slowly, painfully, it began to clear. I saw the stakes for what they were—not just emotional, but existential. This wasn't about romance. This was about survival. About reclaiming my right to live without fear.

Staying single was no longer an option. Not in this twisted reality where danger wore a familiar face and obsession masqueraded as affection. I had to choose a path that felt like betrayal—but only to the ideals I once held in a safer world.

This was war. And in war, you don't always get to fight clean.

So I braced myself. I would gamble with my life—not recklessly, but with calculated courage. Because sometimes, the only way to protect your soul... is to play the game on your own terms.

I decided to dig deeper into the psychopath's brother. What began as a cautious observation soon revealed itself as a potential lifeline. He wasn't perfect, but he was stable enough—a safe spot to hide, at least for the time being.

So I let the rumors spread.

Whispers turned into stories. Stories turned into assumptions. And somewhere in that tangled web, the psychopath must have caught wind of it. His behavior changed almost overnight. He stopped showing up near my neighborhood. No more lurking. No more silent stalking. He began to distance himself, retreating like a predator who'd sensed a trap.

It confirmed my suspicions. He had taken the bait.

Emboldened, I seized the moment. I knew it wasn't the wisest decision. It wasn't clean, it wasn't fair, and it certainly wasn't what I'd imagined for myself. But it was better than the worst that could happen. Better than living in fear. Better than waiting for the next ambush of obsession.

I had chosen survival over purity. Strategy over sentiment. And in doing so, I had bought myself time—time to breathe, to think, to rebuild.

I made my decision, the only way to escape the storm... is to become the eye of it.

Just in few days, my best friend approached me with a message from the psychopath's brother, saying he wanted to talk to me. I was hesitant, and suggested that we shall just leave it for the day. But she insisted, almost dragging me to him. The Psychopath's brother had gathered a massive crowd of friends, nearly half a century's worth. I was shocked by the sheer number of people. Feeling overwhelmed, I repeatedly asked my best friend to let me go. Eager to escape the chaos "I don't want to stand in this huge crowd" I told her, is he crazy? Gathering so many people? But she reassured me "He wants to confess his feelings in front of everyone" I was speechless, unsure how to react.

I wanted to first get him to agree on my plan of fake relationship before he could confess his love, as I didn't wanted him to feel ditched in love. I was neither a cheater nor a liar. So I wanted to speak first. I would lay out the truth—not the emotional truth, but the strategic one. I would explain the danger, the twisted obsession of his brother, the year—long torment I had endured. I believed he would grasp the gravity of it. That he would see beyond the surface and recognize the urgency in my voice.

I didn't wanted him to approach me before I successfully implant my strategy because if he confess before knowing my truth I would have to decline him which would ultimately make me lose my only chance to get rid of psychopath. And if he confess and I accept it without the reality being told to him he might take this relationship seriously which would create further complications. But now I was standing on the edge, I had surpassed the last limit. I hadn't got chance to convey my idea and now the psychopath's brother was standing right in front of me: about to spit out his confession of love, which I desperately didn't wanted to hear from him.

However the though kept haunting me that the psychopath might be waiting for his brother to get rejected so he could pursue me with the triggered intention driven by the revenge. My fear reached all—time high. My inner self warned me against using this false scheme, but my mind, driven by desperation, surrendered to the idea, seeing it as my last chance to escape these terrible clutches.

I was trying my way to reveal the truth to psychopath's brother, but before that could happen I received a phone call from the psychopath's brother's secret girlfriend. It wasn't something new to find out. Finally they were brothers, cheaters, horrible creatures of this world. Knowing his deceitful nature, I drew at the conclusion that these accounts need to be settled exactly the way each one deserved. When the world tries to write you as a victim, you pick up the pen and rewrite the ending.

She was still in love with him.

The secret girlfriend—clinging to a fantasy stitched together by broken promises and selective memory. I could've told her the truth. I could've laid out the facts, the patterns, the betrayals. But deep down, I knew it wouldn't matter.

She would still choose him.

She would still choose to believe in a version of him that didn't exist. A version that whispered love while chasing others. A version that made her feel special while making others feel the same. And that kind of blindness... it wasn't mine to cure.

The fact that he could so callously pursue other girls while promising her love was proof enough. This wasn't a one–time mistake. It was a pattern. A cycle. And she was caught in it—willingly, tragically.

So I chose not to meet her. Not to waste my time. Not to pour truth into a heart that had already decided to suffer in silence.

Because some people don't want rescue. They want the illusion.

And I had no intention of drowning in someone else's denial.

Secondly, such a worthless creature of fraud character does attract fraudulent energies towards them. Hence, I am not guilty of cheating. However, I was aware that if the psychopath's brother were to expose my plan of fake relationship, he would put my life in jeopardy. So my safety was my priority, keeping everything secrete was the solution to the peaceful life. Just a few month, and everything will fall in its place. I believed in my plans, I believed in myself. As the great ancient proverb says 'God helps those who help themselves.' With this, I took control of my situation.

The next few months passed in a strange kind of peace.

Not the peace of freedom, but the peace of a well—maintained illusion. I skillfully kept my distance from the psychopath's brother—close enough to be seen, far enough to remain untouched. It was a delicate dance, and I played my part with precision.

He stayed by my side, unaware of the emotional boundaries I had drawn like invisible walls. I never let him in. Not truly. Because this wasn't a relationship—it was a charade. A shield. A calculated performance designed to convince the psychopath that I was no longer available, no longer vulnerable, no longer his.

And it worked.

The stalking stopped. The lurking faded. The tension that had once wrapped around my days like barbed wire began to loosen. The psychopath kept his distance, watching from afar but no longer approaching. He believed the story I had crafted—and that belief became my armor.

But beneath the calm, I remained alert. Because peace built on illusion is fragile. And I knew that one wrong move, one crack in the façade, could bring the storm crashing back.

So I stayed vigilant. I stayed composed.

Because survival, I had learned, isn't just about escaping danger.
It's about mastering the art of staying one step ahead.

I assumed that the psychopath had moved on, as he was no longer to be seen around me. So, I decide that it was time to come clean and start a fresh, putting past behind me. Over this time, the psychopath's brother had also realized that I wasn't interested in him so he initiated the breakup by proposing one of my classmates, who later confined in me about the offer.

I couldn't help but smile, relived that I was finally free from the situation. It felt like divine intervention, as if God was helping me escape the toxic dynamic. The timing couldn't have been more perfect – it was like killing two birds with one stone.

The stalker had backed off. His brother had moved on. And I was finally free.

Free to breathe.

Free to walk without flinching.

Free to begin again—not as a victim, but as a survivor who outwitted the storm.

The 11th grade was about to end. The final exam had approached. I was breathing fresh air. The last lecture had just finished and my friends were waiting for me at the college gate. So I was in a hurry just when I saw my special one 'Him' walking ahead of me. Spark of joy ignited within me and I couldn't help but wear a gentle smile... which shattered like a fragile glass, plugging me into abyss of terror.

Like a dark specter, the psychopath emerged on the horizon, riding his bike towards me. I stood frozen on the playground as psychopath circled me twice, his bike wheels screeching ominously as he seized me up with an unblinking stare. My feet felt rooted to the spot. Time seemed to slow down as fear wrapped its icy grip around me, leaving me paralyzed and gasping for air.

As the maelstrom of terror swirled around me, my gaze clung to 'Him' trying to reach out for his help, searching for comforting anchor of his presence. But in that shattering moment, he seemed unbothered. He didn't even flinch, didn't acknowledge me. His friends walking along him, however, stared in terror, their mouth wide open to see the incident happening.

His indifference cut deeper than the psychopath's piercing glare.

That unflinching silence, that refusal to even glance in my direction–it shattered something far more delicate than fear. It shattered hope.

I felt abandoned. Betrayed. Not by the one who haunted me, but by the one I had silently trusted to stand beside me when the shadows returned. And in that moment, the fragile thread of our connection—woven through quiet smiles, passing glances, and unspoken warmth—snapped.

No sound. No drama. Just a quiet collapse.

It was the kind of heartbreak that doesn't scream—it just sinks. Like a stone dropped into deep water, vanishing without a ripple. I stood there, frozen in the playground, surrounded by chaos, yet utterly alone.

And I knew then: some silences speak louder than screams.
Some absences cut deeper than betrayal. And some people, no matter how special they once felt, are not meant to walk with you through the storm.

Turbulent emotions bubbled within me — anger, hurt and a deep sense of abandonment. I vowed to excise 'Him' from my memory, to erase his name from my mind like a deleted file. I swore to never again gaze upon his face, to never again feel the sting of his ignorance, I'll forget that I ever loved him**, I no longer know 'HIM'.**

I chose the most powerful act of healing...choosing to forget the ones who chose not to see me.

I wiped away my tears, pulled myself together and walked toward my friends, pretending nothing happed.

A few days later, the air in our colony turned heavy.

News spread like wildfire–an attempted rape had shaken our community. Whispers turned into gasps, and gasps into outrage. I felt the chill of dread creep down my spine as I asked around, trying to understand what had happened.

And then the truth hit me like a ton of bricks.

It was the psychopath.

He had been lurking in our colony for hours–three to four, waiting, watching, calculating. Like a predator circling its prey, he waited for the perfect moment to strike. As evening fell, he spotted a girl walking alone. He tried to grab her, harass her, and drag her into his nightmare.

But she screamed.

Her voice—sharp, terrified, defiant—cut through the silence and summoned help. People nearby rushed in, and he fled. Cowardly. Reckless. Dangerous.

I stood frozen, the weight of it all pressing down on me. This wasn't just a close call. It was a confirmation. A terrifying reminder that my fears had never been exaggerated. That the danger was real. That the storm I had escaped was still raging, just redirected.

As I process this horrific incident, my blood ran cold. I knew that I had been his original target. His intentions were clear. I sensed an even greater danger looming over me, now that his behavior had escalated to such a violent level. The news was flashed in the newspaper in the next few days.

Stepping out of the house became a battle.

The world outside felt hostile, unpredictable. Every street corner whispered danger. Every shadow carried the echo of that nightmarish presence. I wanted to disappear—to lock myself in my room, bury myself in silence, and never step a foot out again.

I was drowning in fear. Not the kind that screams, but the kind that settles in your bones. The kind that makes your breath shallow and your steps hesitant.

But the final exams loomed like immovable mountains. I couldn't afford to miss classes. I couldn't let fear steal my future. So I did the only thing I could—I mustered up the courage, piece by fragile piece, and carried myself through each day.

It wasn't easy. Every morning felt like a war. But I showed up.

Not because I wasn't afraid, but because I refused to let fear win.

And in those quiet victories—walking to college, sitting through lectures, pretending everything was normal—I discovered a strength I didn't know I had. Strength builds not from confidence, but from resilience.

Bravery got redefined in my dictionary: It's the quiet decision to keep going... even when everything inside you wants to surrender and accept defeat.

One morning, the world shifted. I received the news like a slap — sudden, cold, and disorienting. The psychopath was dead.

At first, I couldn't process it. The words felt distant, like they belonged to someone else's story. But my best friend confirmed it, her voice low and trembling. He had died from excessive alcohol consumption. His liver had ruptured. A slow, internal collapse — violent in its own way, but silent, hidden.

But that wasn't the part that made my blood run cold.

What she told me next chilled me to the bone: he had been carrying an acid bottle. He had planned something. Something vicious. Something irreversible.

He had intended to attack.

Moreover, he had been arrested for stabbing a boy with a knife—an act driven, quite predictably, by a dispute over a girl.

Was this his twisted declaration of love—an attempt to show how far he'd go for me? Or was he just rehearsing the same dark role, over and over, in every story he entered?

The thought made my stomach twist. All those moments I had brushed off — the lingering stares, the strange appearances, the way he hovered just outside the edges of my life — they weren't harmless. They were warnings. And I had been walking a tightrope without even knowing it.

I imagined what could have happened. What might have happened. And then I imagined nothing at all — just the silence that followed his death, the eerie stillness of a threat extinguished before it could strike.

It was over. But the fear lingered. Not just of him, but of how close danger had come. How quietly it had crept in. How easily it could have changed everything.

I was frozen in time. Numb to the world around me. My mind reeled, struggling to process the sheer brutality of the psychopaths plan. I was staring death in the face, forced to confront the darkest aspect of human nature. I had narrowly escaped a horrific fate worse than death itself, leaving me breathless, shaken and forever scared.

The news of the Psychopath's death unearthed a long — buried memory. A prophecy that had been foretold to me, dismissed as superstition, now echoed with chilling clarity. I had been warned that I would witness the death of someone who loved me, but that was not all—

A fate sealed a destiny that beckons whispers secret of a future yet to unfold.

A second reunion, forged in the fires of fat, while the ashes of first lay scattered.

Fear's dark whisper warns me away from love's tender flame. Lest I be consumed by the inferno of heartache. To confess my love now would be to invite the cruel hands of faith to snuff out the delicate petals of devotion. I trembled at the thought of surrendering to love's sweet thrall, only to be torn asunder by the merciless tides of destiny.

I was forced to leave in maze, trapped in a never—ending cycle of danger, where survival became the only rule. Every day felt like a repeat of the last: wake up, endure, and pretend. I moved through life like a ghost, disconnected from everything and everyone.

I felt like I was sleep walking through life, unable to truly connect with anyone. Conversations felt hollow, relationships slipped through my fingers like mist. I watched others live while I simply existed.

My future loomed before me like a dark specter, a constant reminder that I was powerless to change the course of my own life. Fear became my inseparable companion. Not the sharp kind that makes you run, but the heavy kind that keeps you frozen. I felt like a bird with wrecked wings—aware of the sky, but unable to reach it. I stopped dreaming. I stopped hoping. I stopped believing that anything could change.

But even shattered wings remember the shape of flight—and I was done forgetting.

5. Forever out of reach.

As I emerged from the shadows of terror, I crumpled to the ground like a wilted flower, drained of vitality. Every breath felt borrowed, every heartbeat a reluctant echo. The trauma hadn't just bruised me–it had hollowed me out. It shattered my faith in friends, family, and even the version of myself I used to trust. I no longer recognized the girl who once believed in safety, in love, in promises that didn't break.

I had been reduced to fragments—memories that stung, hopes that mocked, and a silence that screamed louder than any voice.

Yet, amidst the devastation, a spark within me refused to be extinguished. I knew I had to cultivate my own healing, to nurture my growth. I had to replant my roots in firm ground.

I was a warrior, scarred and battered, but determined to rise from the ashes, I gathered the shards of my shattered self and with painstaking care, I began to reassemble the pieces, to forge a new identity, one that was tempered by the fires of adversity.

My original plan had been simple—at least in theory. I wanted to unburden my heart to *him*. To finally speak the truth about everything I had endured: the harrowing experience, the emotional torment, the way I had been reduced to merely surviving, day after day, under the shadow of someone else's madness. I had rehearsed the words in my mind a thousand times, hoping that by sharing them, I might find peace—or at least understanding.

But that chance dissolved the moment the psychopath died.

With his death came a strange silence. Not relief, not closure—just a heavy, complicated stillness. The kind that made it harder to speak, not easier. A part of me felt sympathy, not for the person he was, but for the soul that had once been human before it twisted into something cruel. It was as if the voices of my ancestors whispered gently, *"Do not speak ill of the dead."* And I listened.

So I stayed quiet.

The truth I had carried for so long—raw, painful, and desperate to be heard—never made it past my lips. It got stuck somewhere between guilt and grief, between fear and forgiveness. And when I tried to speak, all that came out were tears. Silent, unfiltered, and far more honest than any words I could have said. But the future that I read, stole the present from me. I know now—being close to *him* would never be reality, only memory. Because to love *him* is to risk losing *him* and my stars have already whispered the price.

Being the reason for someone's death was heavier than the guilt of simply being alive. It wasn't just grief—it was a haunting awareness that my choices, however necessary, had led to an irreversible end. I didn't set out to destroy anyone. I set out to survive. To protect the one I loved. To shield *him* from the chaos that had already consumed too much of me.

Every move I made was calculated—not out of cruelty, but out of desperation. I played the game because I had no other option. I chose silence when speaking would have endangered us. I chose distance when closeness could have shattered everything. I chose strategy over instinct, because instinct had already betrayed me once.

And yet, when the dust settled and the psychopath was gone, I didn't feel victorious. I felt hollow. The threat was over, but the cost was written in blood and memory. I kept asking myself: *Was there another way? Could I have saved them without losing myself?*

But the truth is, I never had the luxury of clean choices. I had to become something I never wanted to be—sharp, guarded, relentless. Not for revenge. Not for power. But for love. For safety. For survival.

And if that makes me the villain in someone else's story, so be it. I never asked to be the hero. I only asked to make it out alive—with the person I loved still breathing.

People around me who knew about the incident began showing sympathy—soft words, lingering glances, awkward silences. But I never asked for any of it. Their concern, though well—meaning, felt invasive. It wasn't comforting. It was suffocating.

I wanted to move on. To escape that chapter of my life and reclaim some sense of normalcy. But every time someone looked at me with pity, it dragged me back into the very memories I was trying to forget. Their eyes didn't see me—they saw the trauma. The victim. The survivor. And in doing so, they kept the story alive when I was desperate to let it die.

It became more than irritating. It felt like a trap. I had fought so hard to survive, to make impossible choices under unbearable pressure. And now, instead of peace, I was surrounded by reminders—not of my strength, but of my suffering.

I didn't want to be a symbol. I didn't want to be a cautionary tale. I just wanted to be free.

I was done being tagged as the victim. That label, once meant to show compassion, had become a cage. It reduced everything I had endured, every choice I had made, to a single word that didn't fit anymore. I wasn't just someone who suffered—I was someone who survived, who strategized, who protected what mattered most.

I was not responsible for the psychopath's death. He brought it on himself—through his own actions, his own unraveling, his own refusal to stop. His mental instability wasn't mine to carry, and I refuse to wear the guilt that doesn't belong to me.

Yes, I played a strategy. I did what I had to do to survive. To ensure that the chaos didn't swallow us whole. And if that strategy led to consequences, then let it be known: those consequences were born from psychopath's choices, not mine.

I claim my story now—not as a victim, but as the architect of my own survival. I won't apologize for protecting myself. I won't shrink under the weight of others' assumptions.

I stood in the fire and made it out alive. He wrote his ending. I chose mine.

They say survival is instinctive—but mine was deliberate. Calculated. Born not from fear alone, but from the fierce will to live.

I didn't fall into love. I forged a shield. When the threat came—an acid attack attempted, a rape attack narrowly escaped—I didn't crumble. I adapted. The man behind it was no stranger. A psychopath cloaked in familiarity, whose violence simmered beneath a mask of charm. I saw through it. I knew what he was capable of.

And so I did what I had to. I created a diversion. I entered a fake relationship with his brother—not out of affection, but as a strategy. A way to confuse, to deflect, to protect myself. Every smile was armor. Every moment spent with him was a calculated move to keep the predator at bay.

It wasn't easy. The guilt, the fear, the constant vigilance—it wore me down. But I survived. I outsmarted the danger. I walked through fire and came out scarred, yes—but standing.

And when the truth surfaced, when my family learned of the relationship and the breakup, they didn't see the war I had fought. They saw a girl they called *cheap*. They saw sin in my survival. They judged the disguise, not the danger.

They didn't ask for my side of the story. They didn't wonder what I had endured, what I had learned, or how I had survived. Instead, they branded me. As if love, once misplaced, could erase my worth. As if heartbreak was a crime and I was the criminal.

The taunts didn't come in loud accusations. They came in silence—sharp, suffocating silence. In the way they looked at me, in the way they spoke around me. Every slight mistake I made was magnified, twisted into a moral failing. A forgotten chore became a scandal. A moment of laughter was seen as arrogance. I was no longer their daughter, their sister—I was a cautionary tale.

I tried to hold my head high, but the weight of their judgment pressed down like a storm cloud. I wasn't punished for what I did—I was punished for who they believed I had become. And in their eyes, redemption wasn't an option.

But I know what I did. I know why I did it. And I refuse to be ashamed of the choices that saved my life.

This is not a story of romance. It's a story of resistance. Of reclaiming power in the face of terror. Of surviving not just the attack—but the aftermath.

But I didn't take their hurt to heart. I knew they didn't know the whole story. I knew they were reacting to fragments, not the full truth. So I forgave—not because they deserved it, but because *I* did. Because healing meant letting go of the weight they placed on me.

This is not a tale of shame. It's a testament to endurance. To choosing the *bad* when it's *better than worst*. To walking away, not in defeat, but in defiance.

And above all, it's a story of a girl who refused to be ruined.

Now I was in twelfth grade. Life had finally settled into a rhythm that felt safe. My focus was sharp—studies came first, and I was surrounded by friends who genuinely supported me. After everything I'd been through, I had no desire to stand out. I kept my head down, avoided drama, and tried to blend into the background. Attention felt dangerous, like a spotlight that could expose too much.

But the more I tried to stay invisible, the more visible I became.

It started with small things—classmates asking me to join a group singing competition. I hesitated, but their enthusiasm was hard to resist. Then came the dance competition. I tried to say no, but they knew how to tug at my heartstrings, how to make me feel needed. I didn't want to disappoint them. So I said yes.

And something strange happened.

As I stepped onto the stage, as I moved and sang and laughed with them, I felt something shift inside me. A new energy flowed through my wings—not the broken, trembling ones I had carried for so long, but something lighter, stronger. I wasn't just surviving anymore. I was participating. I was living.

The nightmares that had haunted me since the death of the psychopath—the twisted dreams, the suffocating fear—began to fade. Slowly, quietly, they lost their grip. I stopped waking up in panic. I stopped flinching at shadows. I started breathing freely.

For the first time in a long time, I felt good. Not just okay. Not just functional. But truly, deeply at ease. At peace.

But there was one problem, though. Just as I thought I'd broken free, *he* reappeared—the person I had loved quietly, fiercely, since my teenage years. The one I had hidden from the psychopath, not out of shame, but out of protection. He had been my secret sanctuary, a name I never dared speak aloud during the chaos. And now, just when I had begun to feel safe, he returned.

His feelings for me hadn't faded. In fact, they had reignited—stronger, brighter, more intense than before. It wasn't just nostalgia or curiosity. It was real. The connection between us deepened quickly, like roots growing through old soil. It wasn't superficial. It wasn't fleeting. It was the kind of bond that made me feel seen—and that terrified me.

I wanted to keep him away. Not because I didn't care, but because I cared too much. I had survived something dark, something twisted, and I wasn't ready to let anyone close enough to see the scars. I'd tried everything—emotional distance, cold replies, even silence. But he was persistent. His intelligence made him dangerous in a way I hadn't expected. He could read between my words, sense the hesitation behind my smile. He didn't give up.

So I changed tactics.

Being smart wasn't helping me anymore. So I chose to act stupid. I dulled my edges, blurred my thoughts, played the part of someone forgettable. I fumbled through conversations, pretended not to understand, made myself smaller. I hoped that someone as sharp as him would lose interest in someone who seemed foolish, unremarkable, not worth the chase.

Nothing seemed to be working on 'HIM'. At the school entrance, he poured his heart out to me, confessing emotions that left me torn. Knowing the fate that awaits us, I forced myself to drive a wedge between us. I turned him down, feigning disinterest. I anticipated his skepticism, so I resorted to a white lie that I'm not yet over psychopath's brother.

In the moment, I knew I had to shield him from the chaos that would consume us. Though it hurt to let him go, I had to do it to protect him, to spare him the anguish that I couldn't escape. I was being so brutal, not just with him, but more so with myself. The only person I yearned to understand me, was the very one I had to keep at arm's length.

Every cold word, every calculated silence, every moment I pretended not to care—it chipped away at me more than it ever hurt him. I wasn't just shutting him out. I was shutting down parts of myself that longed to be seen, to be understood, to be held without fear.

He was the only person I truly yearned to understand me. Not just the surface, not just the story—I wanted him to see the scars beneath the silence, the strength behind the survival. But I couldn't let him in. Not now. Not after everything.

Not because I didn't love him, but because I did. And love, in my world, had become a dangerous thing. It had been twisted, weaponized, used against me. I couldn't risk letting it bloom again—not when I was still learning how to breathe without flinching.

Keeping him away felt like self—preservation. But it also felt like self—destruction.

I was pedaling against the wind, burning out from inside, trying to flee the emotional inferno that were long held at bay. I wore a mask of composure, smiled when expected, nodded when spoken to, but beneath it all, I was unraveling.

The weight of unspoken pain, of memories I refused to revisit, had begun to rot the edges of my strength. It began to manifest in my physical form, as if my body was screaming for relief from the crippling pain within. The unexpected onset of chickenpox at sixteen was a stark reminder that my emotional hazard had reached the boiling point, and my body was paying the price for the turmoil I'd tried to keep hidden.

A breakdown I hadn't seen coming, but one that made perfect sense in hindsight. My skin erupted in blisters, but it was my soul that felt raw. Every ache, every fevered night, felt like my body screaming what my voice never could: *I'm not okay.* It was as if my body had taken over the burden of grief, of fear, of exhaustion. It had grown tired of waiting for me to speak, to cry, to release. So it spoke for me—in rashes, in weakness, in stillness. I was forced to stop. To lie still. To feel.

And in that stillness, I began to understand.

This wasn't just a virus. This was a reckoning. A physical manifestation of the emotional wounds I had ignored for too long. The trauma I had tucked away, the heartbreak I had silenced, the fear I had swallowed—it had all been simmering beneath the surface, waiting for a crack to spill through.

As I weathered the storm, I realized that my physical suffering was merely a reflection of the deeper wounds I needed to confront and heal. My body broke the silence I was too afraid to shatter.

After nearly a month of isolation and recovery, I returned to school—still a little fragile, but determined to reclaim my rhythm. The corridors felt familiar yet distant, like a world I had watched from behind the glass. And then I saw him.

He was the first person my eyes landed on.

As if drawn by instinct, he turned and saw me too. His expression shifted instantly—tense, alert, flooded with emotion. He started walking toward me, not hurriedly, but with purpose. His eyes searched mine, filled with questions he hadn't yet asked. There was concern etched into every line of his face, the kind that doesn't come from casual curiosity, but from someone who had felt my absence like a wound.

He stopped just short of me, his voice low and careful. "What happened?" he asked, as if the words themselves carried weight. As if he'd rehearsed them in his mind a hundred times but still wasn't sure how they'd land.

I didn't answer directly. I just smiled—a soft, tired smile that held more than words could say. I turned toward the classroom, and as I walked away, one of my friends casually filled in the blank for him. "She had chickenpox. It was pretty bad."

He froze for a second, as if the words didn't register right away. Then his brows furrowed, and he looked at me—not with judgment, but with a kind of startled tenderness.
"Did it hurt a lot?" he asked, his voice low, almost hesitant. There was something raw in the way he said it, like he was trying to imagine the pain I must've endured, and hating that he hadn't known.

Before I could answer, my friend chimed in again, this time with a sharper tone, "Don't you know how dangerous it can be?

He didn't respond immediately. He just stood there, eyes fixed on me, his expression shifting from realization to guilt, his gaze narrowing with remorse. He hadn't known. And now that he did, the weight of not knowing seemed to crush him. He stood there for a moment, as if replaying every day I'd been gone, every moment he hadn't reached out, every time he'd wondered but stayed silent.

There was something raw in his gaze—regret, protectiveness, and a quiet ache. As if he'd failed in some invisible duty. As if he'd been my silent caretaker from afar.

And yet, he didn't chase me. He didn't call out. He just watched me walk away, carrying the knowledge like a secret he hadn't earned.

The year passed by. The 12th grade settled over first class. I was content, I made it. As I stepped into college, I knew I had to make a change for better, to leave the painful memories of the past behind. The pain and trauma I experienced during those times had left an indelible mark on my mind.

I was determined to break free from the shackles of my past and start anew. With the sense of resolve, I made the bold decision to switch colleges; I chose to return to my dream college, seeking a fresh start. This decision proved to be a turning point in my life, as I slowly began to heal and rediscover myself.

Academically, I excelled. My grades reflected the effort I poured into my studies, and slowly, I began to find my footing in the new environment. The textbooks, the lectures, the exams—they gave me structure, a sense of control. But it was beyond the classroom that I truly came alive.

The world of extracurricular opened up like a hidden garden, blooming with possibilities I hadn't dared to explore before. I sang—not just in competitions, but in corridors, in rehearsals, in moments of spontaneous joy. I danced, letting my body speak the emotions I couldn't always put into words. I painted, each stroke a reflection of the colors swirling inside me. And I stood on stages, trembling but determined, as I ventured into public speaking—learning to turn my voice into a tool of expression, not just survival.

Then came the opportunity to become a campus reporter for a local newspaper. It was more than a title—it was a doorway. I began to write not just for myself, but for others. I captured stories, moments, voices. I learned to listen deeply, to observe quietly, and to translate emotion into ink. My words found readers. My thoughts found space.

With each new experience, I felt myself growing—not just in skill, but in spirit. I was expanding, evolving, shedding old fears and embracing new strengths. The girl who once hid behind silence was now speaking, creating, connecting. I wasn't just surviving anymore—I was thriving.

I also began taking tuition classes, initially as a practical step to support my college fees and gain firsthand experience working with children—after all, becoming a teacher had always been my ultimate goal. At first, it was about managing responsibilities and building skills. But as the days passed, something deeper began to unfold.

Each session became more than just a lesson—it was a window into the lives of young minds, each carrying their own fears, dreams, and untapped potential. Watching them struggle through concepts, stumble, and then rise with newfound understanding was profoundly moving. I saw shy students begin to speak up, hesitant learners start to believe in themselves, and once-distracted minds begin to focus with purpose. Their growth wasn't just academic—it was emotional, personal, and transformative.

And somewhere along the way, I realized I wasn't just teaching—I was shaping futures. I was becoming a steady presence in their lives, someone they could trust, and someone who believed in them even when they doubted themselves. The joy of seeing a child's eyes light up with confidence, the pride in their small victories, and the gratitude in their smiles gave me a sense of fulfillment I hadn't anticipated.

This experience redefined my understanding of purpose. It wasn't just about earning or gaining experience—it was about impact. It was about being part of someone's journey, helping them rise, and knowing that in some small way, I had helped them believe in their own strength. Teaching became not just a profession, but a calling—one that continues to inspire and ground me every single day.

As I delved deeper into these activities, something within me began to shift. What started as a means to an end slowly unfolded into a revelation: I was capable of far more than I had ever dared to believe. I was rising—above the clouds of doubt, above the weight of old fears—shattering the illusion that had once kept me small.

Like alchemy, I transmuted my pain into power—not a brittle shield, but a radiant force. The very trials that once threatened to unravel me became the embers that lit my inner fire. Each challenge, each moment of uncertainty, became a stepping stone toward a self I had only glimpsed in dreams.

I faced the unknown not with trembling hesitation, but with a quiet, unwavering resolve. No longer shackled by the fears that once held me captive, I moved forward—braver, bolder, and more resilient than I had ever imagined. My transformation was not loud or sudden, but it was miraculous. It was the kind of miracle that blooms in silence, in persistence, in the choice to rise again and again.

With every step, I felt the weight lift. I felt the air grow clearer. I felt free—not because the world had changed, but because I had. And in that liberation, I found not just strength, but purpose.

My hard work and dedication finally bore fruit when I was awarded the title of *Best Student of the Year*. It was more than just a title—it was a moment that crystallized years of silent perseverance, late—night study sessions, and the quiet battles I fought within myself. When I saw my name in print, etched into headlines and echoed in morning announcements, it felt surreal—like I had stepped into a dream I didn't even know I was allowed to have.

My family's eyes sparkled with pride, their smiles wide and uncontainable. My teachers, who had witnessed my journey from hesitant beginnings to confident strides, showered me with praise that felt both humbling and affirming. And my friends—those who had walked beside me through laughter and stress—looked at me with admiration, not just for the award, but for the journey it represented.

In that moment, I wasn't just being recognized—I was being *seen*. Every ounce of effort, every sacrifice, every time I chose growth over comfort had led me here. And as I stood there, holding that recognition close to my heart, I realized this wasn't the end of a journey—it was the beginning of a new chapter, one where I carried not just the title, but the responsibility and inspiration it symbolized.

As I basked in the warmth of adoration, surrounded by laughter and light, my thoughts drifted—inevitably, irrevocably—to *him*. Not the ghost I had sculpted in my silence, but the boy who once knew me in ways no one else dared to. For the first time in years, I allowed myself to wonder: could we ever be friends again? Could the wreckage of our past be softened into something gentle, something cordial?

Three years. Three long, silent years had passed since our last exchange. And yet, in the midst of joy, I felt a quiet ache—a longing to share my happiness with him. Not out of romance, not out of regret, but from a place deeper, more tender. I wanted him to witness the person I had become. I wanted him to know that I had survived, that I had bloomed.

But I had buried us deep. I had wrapped myself in a shroud of silence so thick, even his persistent attempts to reach me couldn't pierce it. He had tried—oh, how he had tried. He went to every corner of my circle, speaking to our shared relatives, just to prove how much I still meant to him. I had pretended not to recognize his name, his presence. I had erased him so thoroughly; it was as if he had never existed.

And yet, he had. He had existed in every poem I wrote, in every moment of guilt that flickered behind my smile. I had become a phantom in his life, vanishing without a trace, leaving him with no closure, no keepsake, no memory to hold onto. I had denied him even the dignity of goodbye.

Now, as the light poured in and my heart softened, I felt the stirrings of something new. Not reconciliation, perhaps. But recognition. A desire to reach out—not to rewrite the past, but to honor it. To say, *I remember you. I remember us. And I wish you well.*

Would he welcome that? Would he understand the silence not as cruelty, but as a shield I once needed? I didn't know. But for the first time, I was willing to find out

The moment I decided to surprise him at his college felt like a quiet rebellion against the silence I had wrapped myself in for years. I had rehearsed the scene in my mind—his startled smile, the way his eyes might soften with recognition, the possibility of laughter bridging the chasm between us. It was the first time I allowed hope to bloom, fragile and trembling.

But before I could take even a single step toward that reunion, my best friend arrived, her face pale with urgency. The words she spoke shattered everything: *He had met with an accident. He was in the hospital.* Time froze. My breath caught. The world blurred into a haze of disbelief and dread.

I was devastated. It felt as though the universe had intercepted my intentions and responded with a cruel warning. A cosmic whisper: *Stay away*. I couldn't shake the feeling that my thoughts—my longing, my silent prayers for reconnection—had somehow triggered this misfortune. As irrational as it seemed, guilt wrapped itself around me like a second skin. The idea of seeing him, of standing beside his hospital bed, became unbearable. The very thought turned into a nightmare, laced with fear and shame.

Perhaps we were never meant to be. Perhaps fate had drawn a line I was never meant to cross. That day, I made a decision—not out of resentment, but out of a desperate, twisted sense of protection. I disconnected myself from him completely. I withdrew from every shared space, every mutual friend, every thread that could lead back to him. If my absence was the price for his safety, I would pay it without hesitation.

It wasn't closure. It was sacrifice. A quiet surrender to forces I couldn't understand. And in that surrender, I buried not just the possibility of friendship, but a part of myself that had dared to hope.

Some bonds are too sacred to risk, too fragile to hold—so I let go, wondering if my presence might cost him more than my silence ever would. And so I disappeared again, not as punishment, but as protection. Before this love could turn into his ruin, I made my choice—a painful one, maybe even a bad one. But sometimes, *Bad* is better than *Worst.*

6. One Zero One.

While I was still preparing for my final exams, in a surprised twist of fate, I received an offer from a prestigious company based in city. The company's eagerness to have me on board was palpable, and I was presented with an opportunity to join their ranks immediately. Also, they generously offered to grant me a leave of absence to answer my academic exam. Weighing the pros and cons, I decided to seize this opportunity, eager to kick – start my career while also completing my academic commitments.

As I stepped into the uncharted territory of adulthood, I felt the weight of new found responsibilities settling upon me. But the truth was, I was still learning the basics of how to navigate this new world. Overnight, I transitioned from textbooks to boardroom meetings, and a new environment that came with immense pressure and responsibilities.

Gone were the carefree days of college, where I could get away with being a little quirky. Mistakes were no longer being tolerated, and immature behavior was not an option. Every decision I made, every action I took, seemed to carry a high — risk warning label. One wrong move and I could jeopardize not just my future, but also the trust and expectations of my employers. I had to adapt, grow up, and take ownership of my actions. It was a steep learning curve, but I was determined to prove myself. So I embarked on this new journey.

Although my true passion lay in the education sector, I knew that passion alone wouldn't be enough to create the kind of impact I dreamed of. I wanted to be more than just a participant—I wanted to be a force of change, a mentor, a guide. And for that, I needed to grow. I needed to evolve.

So I made a decision: to invest my earnings not in fleeting comforts, but in my future. I began exploring ways to upgrade my qualifications, with a postgraduate program as a potential path. It wasn't just about adding degrees to my name—it was about deepening my understanding, refining my skills, and becoming the kind of educator who could truly inspire.

In that moment, *earning and learning* became more than a mantra. They became my rhythm, my resolve.

Every hour spent working was a step toward a classroom where I could make a difference. Every rupee saved was a seed planted for the future I envisioned.

I wasn't chasing prestige. I was chasing purpose. And with every lesson I taught, every challenge I overcame, I felt myself inching closer to the version of me I had always hoped to become—strong, qualified, and ready to uplift others.

By the time I made my way through the twist and turns of my life, I begin to notice a recurring pattern. Every time I thought I was gaining momentum, building confidence and leaving my past struggles behind, new challenges would emerge, testing my resolve and forcing me to adapt.

This time, the hurdle that loomed on the horizon wasn't danger or heartbreak—it was matrimony. A different kind of storm. One dressed in tradition, wrapped in expectations, and carried forward by well—meaning relatives and family friends who believed they were doing what was best for me.

They came with smiles and suggestions, each one presenting their son like a prize—educated, stable, and "perfect" for me. As if I was a puzzle piece waiting to be placed. As if my story, my scars, my strength, could be matched by a checklist.

I felt like I was being swept into a whirlwind. The world around me spun faster than I could process. Conversations happened without me. Decisions were hinted at, not asked. My silence was mistaken for agreement, my hesitation for shyness.

But inside, I was screaming. Not in rebellion, but in quiet resistance. I had survived too much to be handed over like a token of redemption. I had fought battles no one saw, made choices no one understood. And now, I was being asked to surrender my agency in the name of tradition.

It wasn't that I didn't believe in love or companionship. It was that I needed time. Space. A voice. I needed to choose—not be chosen.

At just 20 years old, I couldn't help but think, "Can't I just catch my breath for a moment?" I was still finding my footing, still learning to capture the complexities of adulthood. The idea of marriage with all its attendant responsibilities and expectations, felt overwhelming, like a weight was being placed on my shoulders before I was ready to bear it.

My parents, however, seemed very eager to move forward—as if marriage were a sale and I was the last item on the shelf before closing time. Proposals started pouring in like monsoon rain, each one accompanied by glowing reviews: "He's well—settled," "He's respectful," "He doesn't drink *too* much," "He's the perfect match!" It felt less like matchmaking and more like a reality show where I was the grand prize.

They'd say things like, *"If the person is good enough, we should prepare for your marriage."* And then the classic line: *"You can do whatever you want after marriage."* As if marriage was some magical portal to freedom. Spoiler alert: it's not. Nobody gets to do *whatever* they want after marriage—unless "whatever" includes negotiating dinner menus, sharing bathroom shelves, and pretending to enjoy cricket matches you never signed up for.

I mean, sure, I could technically do whatever I wanted—like wear glitter eyeliner to breakfast or start a podcast about my in—laws—but I'd also have to survive the emotional Olympics that follow. “Why are you wearing that?” “Why are you going out again?” “Why are you breathing so loudly?”

So while my parents were busy shortlisting suitors like they were picking mangoes at the market, I was quietly resisting the matrimonial tornado. I’d rather be single and sane than married and explaining why I need three hours alone to write poetry and eat chocolate in peace.

Determined to carve out my own path, I pushed back against the pressure to marry, “I’m not ready yet” I insisted. “I need time to focus on my career, to build a life of my own before I take on the responsibilities of marriage.”

Despite my resolve, I knew that my destiny held a different story. It was etched in a different ink. Not the golden script of celebration and union, but something darker, more fragile. Deep down, I was aware that my marriage would be doomed to fail, Prophecy that couldn't be altered. The uncertainties of its duration hang over like a Sword of Damocles. Silent, suspended, always threatening to fall. I didn’t see wedding bells; I saw fault lines. I didn’t dream of companionship; I feared collateral damage.

And so, I made a vow—not to the stars, not to society, but to myself: *I will not marry*. Not out of rebellion, but out of protection. Not for me, but for the soul who might unknowingly walk into ruin.

It was a vow forged in silence. A burden I carried alone. My parents, hopeful and loving, had already consulted priests, astrologers, and cosmic guides—seeking reassurance, seeking signs. They wanted answers. I already had mine.

But how could I tell them? How could I explain that my refusal wasn't defiance, but mercy? That my silence wasn't coldness, but care? That behind every "no" was a prayer for someone else's safety?

One day, as I was walking back to the office from lunch break, near the LIC building I was caught off guard when I saw 'HIM'.

Nothing could have prepared me for the sudden apparition that emerged from the crowd. 'My first love story' was walking towards me. As I caught sight of him almost after four years, I was startled.

He was walking with the tense expression; his eyes fixed on the ground, when suddenly he glanced up, at first, he noticed my colleague walking ahead of me, but as his gaze drifted downward, he caught a glimpse of me. His eyes snapped back up, eyebrows shot up, and a smile crept onto his face – growing wider as the shock gave way to recognition and delight. He quickly raised his head to confirm whether it was really me.

His expression transformed in an instant. The tension melted away, replaced by a radiant smile. He looked stunned, as if he couldn't believe his eyes. I smiled at him and he felt a surge of shyness. His cheeks flushed and he shrank into himself, his eyes searching for ground as shyness washed over him, before he rapidly regained his composer, adopting a mask of confidence.

Our glance clashed and I was lost in the moment. The world around me melted away, living only the two of us, suspended in a timeless bubble. As if the past was not yet done with me. Our smiles mirrored each other's. He seemed to be savoring the moment, his happiness obvious. The transformation was striking –from tense and quiet to happy and radiant. In that instant, he looked more handsome than ever.

Lost in thoughts, I drifted into the office. I felt my defense crumbled. My true emotions lay bare. It was as if he had pierced the veil of my heart, illuminating the secret I had kept hidden. But as reality slowly seeped in, a jarring realization struck me. I shook my head; my hands trembled as it rose to cover my mouth, my eyes widened in horror as I whispered "I messed up". The Pandora's Box lay open in front of the very person who was never, ever supposed to know about it.

The die had been cast, and I felt powerless to stop the chain of events that would soon unfold, events that would bring us together, yet threaten to tear us apart.

I had a plan. Not a Bollywood—style heartbreak saga—just a good old—fashioned cafeteria—level mind game.

Next day, sharp at lunch hour, I strutted into the cafeteria like I was on a mission. Not to eat, obviously. I was there to serve a full plate of *strategic ignorance.* I knew he'd show up. I could practically hear the background music cueing his entrance.

My goal? Pretend he didn't exist. Like, full—on invisibility mode. If he waved, I'd blink at the ceiling. If he smiled, I'd smile at the samosa counter. If he walked past me, I'd suddenly become deeply invested in the texture of my napkin.

I even practiced my "I'm—too—busy—being—important" walk. You know the one—phone in hand, fake laugh with colleague, occasional nod like I'm solving world peace between bites of idli.

I imagined him spotting me, getting all excited, and then—*bam!* Nothing. No eye contact. No reaction. Just me, living my best cafeteria life while he stood there like a confused extra in my movie.

The plan was simple: confuse him, insult him, and make him question every romantic flashback he had. If executed correctly, he'd walk away thinking, *"Was that even her? Did I hallucinate yesterday?"*

And me? I'd be sipping my chai like a villain in a rom—com, silently whispering, *"Mission Ignorance: Accomplished."*

With my script in place, I eagerly awaited the next day, ready to deliver a flawless performance of ignorance.

As I entered the cafeteria, my eyes went full radar mode—scanning every corner, every table, every suspiciously familiar hairstyle. Mission: Spot *him*. But nope. Nada. Not even a shadow. The cafeteria was buzzing with people, but the one person I had mentally rehearsed ignoring like a pro was missing in action.

I waited. One minute. Two. Five. My friends started shifting like impatient toddlers. *"Let's go, we'll be late to office,"* they groaned. I gave them the classic puppy–eyed plea: *"Just five more minutes, please!"* They rolled their eyes. I stood there like a statue of hope. But before I knew it, those five minutes had betrayed me and my friends—bless their dramatic souls—*literally dragged me out* like I was a contestant being evicted from Bigg Boss.

I walked back to the office, head down, sulking. My plan had flopped harder than my attempt to bake cookies last Diwali. I was mentally composing a breakup letter to destiny when suddenly—*plot twist!*

One of my friends leaned in and whispered, *"Hey, the yesterday's guy is checking you out."*

Excuse me, what?!

All my rehearsed indifference, my Oscar–worthy performance of "I don't care," my inner monologue of *"I'm over it"*—flew out the window like a startled pigeon. I instinctively lifted my head and *bam!* Our eyes clashed. And not just clashed—they *high—fived.* With a smile. Like it was hardcoded into our DNA.

He looked at me. I looked at him.

My brain screamed, *"No! Look away! You're supposed to ignore him!"* But my face was like, *"Haha nope, here's a full—blown grin."*

It was chaos. Emotional comedy. A rom—com glitch in the matrix.

He smiled. But not a full, heartwarming, Bollywood—style smile. Nope. It was more like a *"limited edition"* smile—barely there, like his lips were on strike. You could almost hear them say, *"We demand better emotional wages before we commit to a full grin."*

And then—*classic move*—he rolled his eyes at me.

Not just any eye—roll. *The* eye—roll. The one he used to do back in 10th grade whenever I said something in a dramatic mode. That eye—roll had history. It had attitude. It had the power to say *"Oh, you again?"* and

"I'm pretending not to care but I totally do"—all in one smooth motion.

I swear, if eye—rolls were a sport, he'd have won gold medals and a sponsorship deal by now.

And me? I was trying to act cool, like I hadn't just been emotionally ambushed by a half—smile and a nostalgic eye—roll combo. My brain was yelling, *"Stick to the plan! Ignore him!"* but my heart was like, *"Aww, he still does the thing!"*

It was like watching a rerun of my teenage life, but with better lighting and worse emotional control.

So there we were—me, pretending to be emotionally bulletproof, and him, casually tossing eye—rolls like confetti. And somewhere in the background, destiny was probably laughing and eating popcorn.

If and only if I had known that this run—in would be our final act, I would have rewritten this narrative with the ink of second chance. How I desperately wanted to ask him; how had he been for all these years?

I would have told him not to miss me anymore, not to love me anymore and if possible just hate me, if that's what it takes to set you free. You were the dreams of my teenage and passion of my youth, you were my weakness and the core of my strength. You were the reason I learned to feel deeply, to fight quietly, and to protect fiercely. Though my love for you was never ending, I could not let you know it, because this love might have cost your life.

So I choose to let you go. Not with bitterness, but with a quiet kind of grace. I'd rather spend eternity loving you from the shadows, five steps behind you, where you'd never trip over my presence. Where you'd never be endangered by my affection.

7. Faith fights fate.

From the tender age, I was nurtured by my family's loving expectations. They envisioned me as a teacher, as predestined to be one by fate declared by an astrologer to my parents. It deeply ingrained in our families faith. As I grew, this expectation blossomed into a childhood dream and I often imagined myself standing on the podium inspiring young minds,

As a child, I was fortunate enough to spend time at my uncle's place, a man of remarkable intellect and spirituality. Despite his high education and high profile government job, he remained humble and grounded, practicing his faith in the quiet confines of his home. His fascination with palmistry and astrology drew me in, and I would often sit by his side as he delved into the mysteries of the universe. He would regale me with enchanting stories of gods and goddesses, recounting the epic tales of the 'Ramayana' and 'Mahabharata'. These sessions not only sparked my imagination but also laid the foundation of my understanding of the world. My uncle, however, believed that I was too young to grasp the complexities of astrology and Palmistry, and that I was nearly entertained by his stories, as I was only three years old.

Little did he knew, his words were sowing seeds of curiosity in my young mind. As people sought his counsel for astrological guidance, I would listen intently, absorbing the remedies and insight he shared. This exposure ignited a fascination with the interconnectedness of human behavior, karma and the future. I begin to grasp the subtle dynamics of how our actions influence our destiny. While growing up, without my uncle's knowledge, I started to learn the basics of palmistry, intrigued by the lines and patterns that held secrets of an individual's life. This early exposure not only deepened my understanding of the world but also instilled in me a sense of wonder and awe for the mysteries that lie beyond the surface of our everyday life. With this my curiosity to learn and explore kept creatively increasing. My knowledge quota kept vertically expanding, only strengthening my dream goal.

During my childhood days, playtime with the neighbourhood friends took on a unique twist. I would eagerly assume the role of teacher, transforming our makeshift playground into a classroom. My friends would become my students, and I'd delight in teaching those poems, narrating tales, etc. This childhood game was more than just a playful exercise. It was a labor of love. I cherished the opportunity to share my imagination, creativity and knowledge with my friends. As I grave up with the aspiration of becoming a teacher, I naturally develop the essential traits of an educator, including a strong work ethic, effective communication skill and a caring demeanor.

My first year of college marked a significant turning point, as I began taking on tuition classes. This experience proved to be a transformative catalyst, allowing me to sharpen my skills. I discovered a natural aptitude for breaking down complex concepts into accessible, bit – sized pieces, making learning a seamless and enjoyable experience for my students.

As word of my tutoring prowess spread, I earned a reputation as a reliable and effective teacher in my neighbourhood. Parents begin to entrust me with their children's academic development, sending them to me with unwavering confidence. This vote of confidence not only bolstered my self—assurance but also depend my conviction that I would really be one of those great once 'The Teacher' one day.

I had meticulously charted my career trajectory, balancing my work at the insurance company, the one I had joined during my college, In order to invest my earning in my post graduate studies. However, fate intervened, and my plans took an unexpected turn. When I saw "Him" again, after so many years at the cafeteria, I couldn't help but think — can I not alter my predetermined path? Can I not change the course of my destiny that has been ordained for me? I kept pondering; what if I choose a different route? What if instead of pursuing education I continue down the insurance path? If only I can alter my career from a teacher to be, to just an employee in the insurance sector. Maybe, just maybe, this change would grant me a second chance to be with him by changing the fate.

Few weeks later, I got a call from my professor. He suggested getting me enrolled in a PG program that would qualify me to become a college level professor. Recognizing the immense potential this opportunity held, my professor enthusiastically encouraged me for the same. With conviction, my professor approach my parents, he persuaded my mother and won over her confidence to send me with him for answering the exam that was supposed to be held in Bangalore city. But I choose silence. As a new plan had begun to take shape in my mind. I was hallucinating; should I abundant my long awaited career now that opportunity had finally arrived or should I gamble on it by changing the rout to my career.

Like a shipwrecked sailor, clinging to the splinters of his shattered vessel, I clung to the wreckage of my dreams—weathered, bruised, but still afloat. The tide was merciless, the horizon uncertain, yet I held fast to the hope that I could alter the course of my life. Not drift. Not drown. But steer.

This decision was not taken lightly. I knew what I was risking: the comfort of a secure future, the quiet nods of family approval, the safety of a path already paved by others. I was walking away from the known, from the predictable rhythm of expectations, into a storm of possibility.

In that moment, I surrendered—not in defeat, but in defiance. I embraced the unknown, not as a threat, but as a promise. A blank map. A portal. A dare.

I gave it my all. Every ounce of my being, every breath, every heartbeat became fuel for this quest to redefine my fate. I was no longer waiting for destiny to arrive—I was chasing it, teeth bared, eyes blazing.

Driven by an insatiable desire—not for glory, not for applause—but for agency. For the right to choose.

The outcome may be uncertain, but one thing was clear— I might rise or fall, and if I failed? Let it be spectacular. Let it be mine. But I will never surrender to the dictates of predetermined destiny. I wanted to give myself an opportunity to know that I had left no stone unturned, and that I'd tried everything possible so I could move forward without any regrets.

When I declared my final decision not to enroll in the competitive exam, my mother was devastated, and my sister criticized me, mocking my choice and saying I was squandering a valuable opportunity. They ridiculed me, claiming I wasn't taking life seriously. My professor was equally disappointed. Having genuinely believed I had the potential to excel in the exam. Despite his initial persistence, he eventually gave up on me and showed no further concern, clearly hurt by my decision.

I had hoped that my decision to continue working at the insurance company would be the right one and that I would continue to thrive there. However as the deadline for the enrollment of exam passed, things took a drastic turn. My career at the insurance company began to turn Topsy—turvy.

I found myself facing a series of challenges with atmosphere at the office becoming increasingly toxic. Suddenly, my colleagues became hostile towards me. A friend I had considered like an elder sister made a critical error by depositing a post— dated cheque in the bank, but when questioned by management, she shifted the blame on me, claiming it was my department's responsibility. I was taken aback, wandering why she would betray me like that; when she clearly knew that it was not at all my fault. This was a devastating blow, not only to my professional career but also to our personal relationship.

Within a few weeks, the air around me began to shift. Whispers replaced greetings. My colleagues, once cordial, now treated me like an outcast—like I had trespassed into a space I was never meant to occupy. The warmth drained from the room, replaced by cold glances and calculated silences.

The situation escalated quickly. I was instructed to stay late at the office—contrary to what was promised in my employment contract. Initially, they assured me it was only until 8:30 p.m., just once a month, to upload documents to the Delhi office. But soon, that promise dissolved. My manager informed me that I would need to stay late whenever "work demanded it." And work, it seemed, demanded everything.

Night after night, I found myself trapped in the office until 8:30 p.m., the fluorescent lights flickering like warnings. The commute home became a gauntlet. The local bus, dimly lit and crowded with shadows, felt more perilous than ever.

One night, I discovered my dupatta had been slashed—razor clean. Another time, a piece of chewing gum was stuck to my shoulder. It wasn't clumsy. It was deliberate. A quiet act of harassment. A message.

I felt it in my bones: I never belonged there.

This wasn't just a job. It was a slow erosion of dignity. A place where silence was expected, and resistance punished. I began to rethink everything. The dream. The sacrifice. The gamble.

Was this the cost of ambition? Or had I mistaken a trap for a ladder?

Though not immediately, the thought began to settle in—a quiet whisper at first, then a steady echo. I began to consider quitting my job. Not out of weakness, but out of wisdom. I realized this path, no matter how long I walked it, wouldn't propel me forward. It was a treadmill disguised as a staircase.

And yet, I found solace in knowing I had tried. I had shown up, endured, given it my all. That mattered. That counted.

In a twist of poetic justice, the former colleagues eventually faced consequences that mirrored their own misdeeds. One falsely accused me of misplacing a bank cheque, only to be later terminated for actual fraud—an ironic vindication. The other, a manager who broke her promise about work hours and routinely demanded late nights, found herself in a new job where she too was misled—promised a desk role but assigned fieldwork instead. It was as if the universe had quietly returned the favor.

Slowly, I became convinced that the course of my destiny was unchangeable—not in a tragic way, but in a way that felt strangely liberating. I had made the right decision by distancing myself from *him*—the shadow that lingered, the voice that once felt like fate.

But he refused to halt.

8. A fake deal.

Even before I turn 21, marriage proposals started flooding in. It was overwhelming, to say the least. The news about this tragedy spread through my office and social circle. At work, I found myself being discreetly asked about whether I was interested in settling down. Some colleagues would casually mention that they knew of a 'great catch' or a 'perfect match' for me, while others would more boldly express their own interest in marrying me. I tried to handle each situation with tact and diplomacy, politely declining each proposal and explaining that my family adheres to traditional norms and that they are searching a groom within our community.

Amidst the flurry of marriage proposals, I was taken aback by the sudden interest shown by this one person. To my surprise, one of our distance neighbors, a close friend of my mother began showing interest in me. My mother, who's always been found of him, would often invite him over. I had known him since my 11 standard, but his shady character kept me from befriending him. I refused to even know him. He had a reputation for being a ladies man, with multiple girlfriends and a history of cheating. Despite this he'd been dating a girl for past seven years then, promising to marry her or so she claimed. But promises from him were like smoke: visible for a moment, then gone.

When he started visiting my mother attempting to ingratiate him with my mother since my first year of college, I maintained a safe distance. Even back then, I'd mealy acknowledge him with a brief smile before walking away. His history had preceded him, and I'd never had any interest in pursuing a friendship with such a man but when he approached me, his audacity left me speechless.

I was about to rebuke him for asking me out. But then, a thought crossed my mind. Given my fate that my marriage would end in devastation, I wonder if this person might be the one I could marry without feeling guilty. Having ruined the lives of so many innocent girls, he doesn't deserve a good life. Now that I know that I hold no powers to decide upon what one deserves or not, but at that age and with that kind of anger issues, that’s how I processed my thoughts.

I hesitated, and instead of rejecting him outright, I told him that I’d consider his offer if my parents approve it.

This unexpected turns of event left me questioning my own motivations and the fate that seemed to be unfolding before me.

As I've always believed, only equals can truly walk side by side.

He was never worthy of someone so unblemished, so pure in spirit. We were misaligned from the start.

And when despair whispered its final lullaby, I stood at the edge of the cliff, ready to surrender. But the divine had other plans. My sincerity, my quiet acts of goodness — they did not go unseen. Instead of falling, I was lifted. Not into oblivion, but into grace. Cloaked in dignity, crowned with honor, the edge that once threatened to consume me became the very place I learned to fly.

He walked away with rejection and I was safe again.

Looking at the past few events, I couldn't help but wonder why people are drawn to me, despite my unassuming appearance. I'm just an average looking girl with a simple style, no fancy makeup. I don't fit the mold of the modern glamorous ideal. While chatting with a friend I simply questioned one of my close girls and her response surprised me. "It's not about your looks dear; it's about your behavior. Your kindness, politeness, the way you clearly define your boundaries, no nonsense, strong character. That's what attracts people towards you. If I were a boy I would have definitely fallen for you".

Oh! So that's where the problem lies. I should work upon being 'not so nice person'. Because apparently, being kind is magnetic. Being clear is captivating. And being strong is...misinterpreted.

Funny, isn't it? You build yourself with grace and grit, and suddenly you're the flame everyone wants to touch.

But I'm not here to be admired. I'm here to be *understood.*

With this new plan, I began to act out.

I snapped at people for no reason. Rolled my eyes at well—meaning advice. Stirred gossip like it was tea. I wore my irritation like armor, hoping it would make me unapproachable, undesirable—untouchable.

Ironically, it worked. The very people who had been waiting for an excuse to criticize me now had their ammunition. I handed it to them, gift—wrapped in sarcasm and silence. Let them talk. Let them judge. Maybe then, the proposals would stop. Maybe then, I could breathe.

I pretended to be difficult. Cold. Aloof. Not because I wanted to hurt anyone—but because I didn't want to lead anyone on. I didn't want to be the reason someone hoped, only to be disappointed. So I chose the villain's mask. It was easier than explaining the truth.

But someone saw through it.

She didn't confront me with anger. Just quiet clarity. Her words struck like a stone skipping across still water, each ripple deeper than the last.

"You know what?" she said. "A bad person has no limits to their bad behavior. Because they don't care. They don't cry in hiding. But someone with a kind heart—pretending to be bad—will never cross certain lines. They can't bring themselves to hurt others. And I know what you're trying to do."

I froze. Because she was right.

I *had* cried in hiding. I *had* hesitated before every sharp word. I *had* drawn invisible lines I couldn't bring myself to cross. Because deep down, I wasn't trying to destroy anyone—I was fed up of being termed as nice and chased after.

But kindness, even when disguised, has a scent. And some people can smell it through the smoke.

She understood me well. I felt deep sense of caring. Oh! So dearly I wished to hug her and give way to all my worries in the form of tears. If only I could talk out my inner self to her. I felt like to melt down in her arms and let her rebuilt me in a better version of me. For I knew my intentions were misaligned. Pretending to be someone that I'm not was suffocating. Each passing day was reminding me that I was living a lie. The ache within me grew a relentless longing to shatter the facade and unveil my true self.

But the fear of tomorrow's consequences held me captive. Sacrificing present was the only way out for a regretless future.

One evening, after a long day at the office, I returned home expecting the usual quiet comfort. But as I stepped through the door, I noticed a man sitting with my father in the living room. They were laughing heartily, as if sharing stories from a time long past. I greeted the man politely, though his face didn't stir any recognition in me, and I walked into the house, brushing off the encounter as one of my father's many acquaintances.

Moments later, my mother called me into the kitchen. Her tone was curious, almost teasing. "Do you know who's sitting with your father right now?" she asked. I shook my head, genuinely unsure. She looked surprised, even slightly amused, and continued, "He's the father of your classmate from tenth standard. You two went to college together too. You were good friends."

Her words struck me like a distant echo—familiar yet unreachable. I frowned, trying to summon a memory, a face, a moment. Nothing came. "Why is he here?" I asked, my voice tinged with unease. My mother, now more serious, replied, "He's come with a marriage proposal. For his son."

A marriage proposal? For me? From someone I couldn't even remember?

Then she mentioned his name. It sounded hollow, like a name I should know but couldn't place. My mother looked at me again, puzzled. "You don't know him? Are you sure?" she asked, twice. Her insistence made me feel even more lost. He claimed to be my friend. A friend I had apparently shared years of life with. But my mind was blank.

I turned away, retreating to my bedroom. My steps felt heavy, as if the air around me had thickened. My thoughts were tangled. I sat on the edge of the bed, numb. Tears welled up in my eyes, uninvited and unexplained. Why was I feeling this way? Why couldn't I remember someone who had once been close to me?

Was it just forgetfulness? Or was there something deeper—something buried, something I had chosen to forget?

In those few minutes, the memories that had consumed me since my teenage years were eclipsed. The one I woke up thinking about, the one, whose presence breathed life into my every waking moment, I forgot 'Him'?

What had just happened? I rushed out into the sitting room. His father had already left, probably have felt insulted. Was this the destiny's cruel twist, eerily wiping away my memories? So also the thought of being with him was a bittersweet serenade, a melody that filled my soul with joy, yet echoed with the haunting refrain of our inevitable good bye. Every moment we shared would be stolen glances at happiness, a fleeting whisper of what could never be.

After the incident, the days blended together in a haze. I was consumed in guilt for rejecting him in such a harsh way. Despite my doubts, I couldn't help but wonder, was this the only way it could have ended. The more I thought about the situation, I couldn't shake off the feeling that fate had dealt me a cruel hand. What sin had I committed to deserve such a dramatic and heart—wrenching turns of event. All I ever wished was a simple life, free from complications. I didn't aspire to luxury or grandeur. My one desire was to be with him – the person I've loved since the very beginning. I was willing to give up on anything and everything for just one chance to stand next to him.

I thought I had hit the rock bottom but this was not the end. Few days later, one night, I received a call from an unknown caller. The person's voice on the other line was barely above the whispers, trembling with each word as he struggled to hold back emotions. The tone was laced with desperation. Each breath was audible, a ragged, shaky sound that conveyed the depth of his distress. The words were fragmented, punctuated by pauses and sniffling sound, as if he was fighting to compose himself. The silence between the words felt heavy. Despite the physical distance, the emotional pain was almost tangible, transmitting through the phone, like a raw, unfiltered current. His emotions clashed like tsunami waves "I really... really love you yaar. I'm begging you just meet me once." He tried every avenue, conveying his emotions, hoping against hope that he might convince me.

We had never truly met to call it a meeting. We never even had a talk to call it a conversation and we never stood together as two people in love. All I remember is running away from him, desperate to escape his gaze and avoid him. But I knew that if I gave in to him this time, I will never be able to return. So, I stood stone firmed listening to his every word, though each one chipped away at my resolve, making me weak, but without hesitation, I gathered the strength to say "I don't know you. Don't ever call me again." I ended the call.

My mother had been calling out to me to dine with them. How could I have faced them with tears streaming down my face? I had nowhere to hide, nowhere to crash. When she kept asking me to come out, I made up an excuse, yelling that my stomach hurts and that I'm going to bed. I curled up in the blanket. My head throbbing with his thought. How was he coping? Was he okay? Was someone with him to watch over him? I worried sick. Fearing he'd make a desperate mistake. I had already seen one death.... Want to see no more. My mind was a maze of worst–case scenario. These thoughts kept me haunting all night. I searched for the pain killer in my father's medical pouch, but found none. The headache was unbearable. All night I banged my head on floor, desperate to escape the anguish that threatened to consume me.

I knew that I needed closure to this story, and I also knew that he wouldn't give up so easily. He'd been pursuing me since school, eight years from then and I feared he'd stop at nothing. Desperate to protect him, I made another bad decision. I deliberately pretended to be interested in that one fraud—characterless person, hopping he'd be repelled by my choice. My only concern was his safety, no matter the cost it might cause to my reputation.

Within some days I received a confirmation that my plan was a success. One of my distant neighbors who was a common friend met me on the way back home. She informed me that 'He' met her asking if I'm seeing someone at work and she confirmed his suspicions. I felt a wave of relief. Knowing that the news had reached him, I hoped that this would be the final blow and he would give up on me completely. My strategy worked well, and I never heard from him ever since.

I buried my love covered with the soil of fate. But instead of withering away, it silently flourished. Unseen and unheard by the world, it continued to grow, a secret garden of devotion.

No one knew. Not even him.

He was chasing fire—reckless, radiant, impossible to hold. And I was the storm he didn't see coming. The complication he never asked for. I knew I was the problem. The detour. The ache he couldn't name.

But still, he ran toward me. And I stood still, knowing that if he reached me, he'd burn. And I'd burn with him.

Some people are born under lucky stars. I was born under a sky that never cleared. A fate stitched with unfinished stories and love that never quite made it to the surface.

But reality had other plans.

And so I live with this garden inside me—blooming in silence, thriving in sorrow. A love that never died, only learned how to live without being seen.

We were two forces in motion—equal in intensity, opposite in direction. He moved toward me with purpose, each step a declaration of hope, of longing, of belief that love could still be salvaged. And I? I moved away with equal force, driven by fear, by memory, by the quiet certainty that closeness would undo me.

It wasn't indifference. It was protection.

He chased with open hands, I fled with clenched fists. He offered warmth, I wore armor. Every effort he made to reach me was met with my silent rebellion, a refusal to be seen, to be touched, to be known.

We were testing something fragile. Not just love—but fate. Timing. Will.

And in that test, we became reflections of each other's extremes. He, the flame. I, the wind.

In the end, love bowed to fate.

He, with all his efforts, had to let go. Not because he stopped loving, but because he loved too much to keep chasing someone who kept slipping through his fingers. And I? I lost my battle—not with bitterness, but with grace. I stood tall, even as my heart crumbled quietly beneath the weight of goodbye.

It wasn't a war of anger. It was a dance of devotion—he reaching, I retreating. Each step a testament to how deeply we felt, and how deeply we knew we couldn't last.

It wasn't weakness. It was choice.

A choice to protect him from the venom I knew I carried. A choice to let go before the damage became permanent. A choice to lose with grace, even when my heart screamed for mercy.

He resigned with silence. I surrendered with dignity.

But in that surrender, I loved him more than ever. Not in the way that demands presence, but in the way that lets go—for his peace, for mine. I watched him disappear into the distance, and though my soul ached to call him back, I whispered to the wind instead.

Some loves aren't meant to be lived out loud.
Some are meant to bloom in the quiet corners of the heart,
Where they remain untouched, eternal, and achingly beautiful.

9. The complete surrender to the will of the unknown.

I was born under a shadow the stars refused to lift. An astrological curse, they called it—*Manglik.* Not mild, not negotiable, but strong. Strong enough to cast doubt on every promise of love. Strong enough to make even fate hesitate.

They said my presence could bring ruin to the one who chose me. That my stars were misaligned, my fire too fierce, my energy too volatile. I wasn't just marked—I was warned against. A danger wrapped in devotion.

And so, every time love approached, it came with caution. With rituals. With remedies. With fear.

I watched others fall into love like rain—soft, natural, unquestioned. But mine came with thunder. With charts. With whispered concerns behind closed doors.

I didn't ask for this. I didn't choose it. But I carried it. Quietly. Like a poison in my veins. Like a truth I couldn't rewrite.

I had always been resistant to the idea of marriage and I tried my best to convince my parents that I was not interested in any of the proposals. However, my mother was desperate to get me married off, largely due to concern about my younger sisters. Despite my reservations, she went ahead and finalized the arrangement without my consent.

My uncle, my mother's elder brother, had actually warned her about to be groom's bad family reputation, she still insisted on going onboard with the same proposal. Dismissing it all, clinging to the hope that this match would solve more than just my future—it would ease the path for my sisters too.

Perhaps, I thought, this was a sign that I should trust my instinct. I chose to quietly follow my mother's wishes, surrendering to the circumstances that had been set in motion. I was forced into this union, not by love, but by expectation. My silence was mistaken for consent, and my heart was never asked.

I tried to meet up with the groom before marriage to give him prior—information about the 'kundali dosha' that I'm having; that I'm a strongly mangalik persone and this could have adverse effect on his health, but his mother advised him not to have this meeting. Subsequently, they informed my parents that the kundalis were compatible and that the marriage could proceed without concern.

I found it doubtful as none of the proposals had confirmed matching the groom's kundali with mine before this one. This piece of information was felt relaxing. Within a month, I was married off. I didn't even have a chance to process my emotions, but it wasn't a joyous occasion for me. I felt powerless to change the course of events. It was as if my life's script had already been written and I was merely following the narrative. I was left with no choice but to surrender to the consequences and accept the will of the universe.

To my surprise, the person I married turned out to be exceptionally kind and good—natured individual, with down—to—earth and uncomplicated personality that I adore. His gentle and polite demeanor, with a tender and soft—hearted nature, combined with his devotion to god and respect for rituals was truly heartwarming. As I got to know him better, I felt a deep sense of sympathy and kindness towards him. What struck me most was his high standard of respect towards women.

Life was cruising along smoothly, and year had passed since the marriage. Everything seemed perfect, until one fateful day he met with a major accident. Thankfully he was unharmed, but the incident made me relate it to as a sign of impending doom. I was terrified of losing him. And the thought that my fate was somehow intertwined with his was unbearable.

Desperate to prevent any harm from befalling him, I turned to every possible remedy. I fasted, prayed, and visited sacred places, seeking solace in the traditions and rituals passed down by our ancestors. I even urged my husband to join me in these efforts, without letting him know my true concern, as I didn't wanted him to get worried, hoping that our combined prayers might be heard by the almighty.

The causes of his accidents were eerily unusual, sometime; a dog would dart across his path. Other time a buffalo would suddenly appear. On one occasion, a snake slithered onto the road, causing him to lose balance and fall. It was as if nature itself was conspiring against him, with natural obstacles inexplicably getting in his way. Each incident left me feeling increasingly anxious; wondering what was behind these strange events.

As the accidents continued to occur at the alarming rate, I found myself on the quest for answers, delving into the realm of astrology, numerology and many more, in a bid to unravel the mystery behind this persistent curse. Driven by a sense of desperation and determination, I sought to decipher the cryptic message hidden within the stars and numbers, hoping to uncover the underlying causes of these calamities.

My search for solution let me down the path of spiritual seeking, as I endeavored to understand the karmic forces that seemed to be at play. I was resolute in my pursuit of knowledge, poring over ancient text and seeking guidance from experts in the field, all in the hopes of finding a way to break this curse and defy the fate.

One rainy morning, while I was getting my daughter ready for her school, I got a phone call. The person on the phone asked for my husband. I was little surprised as why someone would call me and ask about my husband because none of his colleagues or friends or even his family had my contact details with them – I had always kept a low profile. So I questioned the person on the phone about getting my number. I was horrified at his answer when he told me that he got the number from my husband's cell phone and that he was being taken to the hospital for treatment. The person further informed that he met with a major accident early that morning while riding with his friend who had been also hospitalized. A cryptic warning whispered in my ear 'the fate will show its face soon, the time is running out, the clock is ticking.'

I felt utterly drained of energy upon receiving the devastating news. In a state of despair, I instinctively sought solace in the sacred space of our home temple, where the serene presence of lord Ganesha's idol beckoned me. Overwhelmed with emotions, I collapsed at the feet of the deity, unable to articulate my anguish in words. All I could do was surrender to my tears, letting them flow uncontrollably as I sought comfort and protection in the divine presence. Time stood still as I sat there consumed by grief. My daughter's school hours had passed. Her school bus honked twice or thrice may be and it went off as I did not respond, my daughter came to me telling about the same and that she want to go to school but I was too numb to reply her questions.

Just then my husband called up. I grasped at the phone desperately, all awake. He softly talking said "Don't worry, I'm fine. I'm coming home now." A complete silence engulfed around me. Feeling relieved I waited for his arrival.

He was advised by the doctor to take rest to recover from internal swelling. His employer also provided him with the much needed break. During this convalescence period, it was highly emotional to see a steady stream of friends visiting to check on him. It was truly touching to witness the outpouring of care and concern from his loved ones, who rallied around him with kindness and support. I never knew that he was so popular.

Fourteen years have passed now, though life has been good to us, but a clinging sense of unease persists, a nagging feeling that the fat is watching and waiting.

I had exhausted every avenue, pushing myself to the brink of collapse in my quest to find a solution. Desperate to alter the course of events and change the destiny that seemed to be unfolding, I had left nothing undone in my limits to protect this family. Yet, despite my herculean efforts, every door I knocked on let to a dead end, every remedy I tried proved ineffective, and every plea I made seemed to fall on deaf ears.

The crushing reality began to sink in. I had reached the limits of my powers, and I couldn't stop but to think why must the innocent suffer? Why such a godly person, a beautiful soul destined for such a tragic fate that future hold? But the universe always seeks balance, balance of justice. And I got a chance to understand the ultimate rout that universe follows to maintain this justice.

I received an unexpected phone call from a woman. As it turns out, I had been tutoring her nephews, and she had heard about me from them. What she revealed after that left me stunned. She shared a heartbreaking account of how my mother—in—law had ruined her life and the extent of her malevolent influences. As I listened, I couldn't make sense of my own emotions; shocked, disgust and a deep sense of sadness. The more I learned from neighbors and relatives, the more I realized that her involvement in illicit activities was not just a one—time mistake but a pattern of behavior that spanned decades, from her teenage years to the present day, she had been causing harm and destruction to those around her.

This made me think about my husband's past and the kind of environment he grew up in. despite being a kind and pure, he was born to a woman who had brought suffering to countless life. It's ironic that it wasn't just fate that brought me into this family but it's more like the universe sought to balance the scale, bringing light and devotion to counteract the shadows of evil, as the saying goes ' opposite attracts'.

My husband once shared his childhood memory, at just seven years old; he had performed his first fasting and puja. It was the same year that I was born. He would sometime humorously say it as I'm his reward. But I'm never been one to seek praises or pride myself, for I knew my own limitations and flaws. However, when my husband expresses his gratitude for having me as his life partner, it fills me with a sense of purpose and fulfillment. He often tells me that I am his heaven and those words make my heart swell with joy and contentment.

Although, the definition of love is difficult in my dictionary, but I dedicated my life to my husband's well—being, made sacrifices for our benefit and tirelessly worked towards our happiness. With every fiber of my being, I strove to be his rock, his confident. I selflessly put his needs before mine, ensuring that he felt loved, valued and cherished. My commitment to him was unwavering and I took pride in being his partner in every sense of word.

10. The sixth sense: Intuition Beyond the powers of reality.

In the realm of my inner vision, a poignant prophecy unfolds with a haunting clarity. Like a mirror reflecting the depth of my soul, I behold a future scene that is at once eerily familiar and heart—wrenchingly unknown.

The landscape of this impending reality remains shrouded in mystery. Yet the faces that populate it are disturbingly dear to me. The occasion that is about to transcript is a sorrowful one, a heartbreaking convergence of circumstances that threatens to shatter the very foundation of my existence. And yet, I'm drawn to this calamitous event with a morbid fascination, like a moth helplessly attracted to the flame that will consume it.

The canvas of fate has already been stretched,

The frame of destiny already hung upon the wall.

All that remains is for the brushstroke of time,

To reveal the masterpiece of misery that awaits me.

Two years from now, a mere blink of the cosmic eye, separates me from this looming cataclysm. My heart trembles with trepidation as I contemplate the inevitability of this fate. I am torn asunder by the conflict desire to flee from this dreadful destiny and to stand frozen in time, suspended in this fleeting moment of relative tranquility.

Each passing day feels like a grain slipping through the hourglass — silent, irreversible, and cruelly indifferent. The future looms like a shadow cast by a storm yet to arrive, and I find myself paralyzed between resistance and surrender. There is a strange serenity in knowing the end, yet a maddening ache in not knowing how to meet it. I am both the prisoner and the prophet of my own unraveling.

And yet, somewhere beneath the dread, a flicker of defiance stirs. Perhaps fate is not a fixed script but a challenge — a mirror held up to my soul, daring me to rewrite the ending. Perhaps this moment, this breath, this heartbeat, is not a pause before collapse, but the beginning of a quiet rebellion.

Oh! For the power to arrest the passage of time, to freeze the clocks relentless tick—tock and preserve this fragile instant of peace. If only I could stretch this moment into eternity, cocooned in its stillness, untouched by the chaos that looms. For in the depths of my soul, I know — I am not ready. Not ready to face the trials that lie ahead, not ready to confront the darkness that gathers like a storm on the horizon of my existence.

The future feels like a beast pacing just beyond the veil, its breath hot with inevitability. I stand here, trembling — not from cowardice, but from the sheer weight of knowing. Knowing that the path forward is carved in stone, yet my feet remain bare and bleeding. I long to retreat into the sanctuary of now, where the air still holds a whisper of hope, where my heart still dares to dream.

But time is merciless. It does not pause for pleading hearts or trembling hands. It marches on, indifferent to the fragility of human resolve. And so I gather my fragments, piece by piece, praying that when the hour strikes, I will not shatter — but rise.

Though the future's blueprint unfolds before me like smoke in the air, I choose to ignore its revelation, embracing instead the beauty of the present. With a bright smile and a happy heart, I'll cherish every moment that comes my way, for I know that destiny's course is unstoppable and the wait is inevitable. I elect to cherish every fleeting moment, to seize the beauty of the present, and to transform each day into an unforgettable masterpiece. I choose not to be shackled by the chains of worry, nor be paralyzed by the uncertainty of tomorrow.

Instead, I choose to anchor myself in the here and now. I focus on the canvas of today, painting it with vibrant colors of joy, gratitude and love. I strive to live each moment with intention, to breath in its beauty and to savor its sweetness. In this way, I transform the uncertainty of tomorrow into the promise of today. I trade the anxiety of the unknown for the peace of the present. And I discover that, even in the face of destiny's unyielding course, I have the power to choose to smile, to choose to be blissful.

And so, I walk forward – not with the burden of what might be, but with the quiet strength of what is. The present becomes my sanctuary, a sacred space where fear loses its grip and hope takes root. I no longer chase the illusion of control over the future, nor do I mourn the ghosts of the past. Instead, I gather the light of this moment, however fleeting, and let it warm the corners of my soul.

Each sunrise is no longer a countdown, but a gift – a fresh canvas awaiting the brushstrokes of my intention. I greet the day not with dread, but with reverence. I laugh more freely, love more deeply, and listen more closely to the whispers of my own heart. In choosing presence, I reclaim my power. In choosing joy, I rewrite the narrative.

Destiny may chart its course, but I – I choose how to sail. And in that choice, I find liberation. I am not merely surviving the storm. I am dancing in the rain.

11. Glimpses of glory.

As I meander through the labyrinthine corridors of my life. I find myself pondering the mosaic of memories that will eventually become the narrative of my existence. I am driven by an insatiable desire to weave a story that is replete with purpose, passion and profound sense of fulfillment. I have created a history that I can look back on with pride and no regrets. I have crafted this life with humbleness and truthfulness, striving to remain genuine and taking every measure to ensure the well—being and safety of those around me.

I have always held the quiet conviction that a life well—lived is not measured by the weight of gold or the grandeur of possessions, but by the depth of one's character and the warmth one leaves behind in the hearts of others. True fulfillment, I believe, lies not in the pursuit of luxury or the applause of the world, but in the gentle art of being useful — of showing up in someone's life as a source of light, comfort, or strength. To make a meaningful difference, even in the smallest way, is to leave a legacy that no riches can rival. I strive to walk my path with integrity, to offer kindness without condition, and to shape my journey with purpose. In my own quiet, imperfect way, I aim to be a ripple in someone's still water — a reminder that goodness, though often unseen, is never wasted.

When students reach out to me, sharing their stories and reflections, I'm reminded that my past, though simple, has been meaningful and impactful and true to my values.

I've got this one life, but I chose to multiply this life in thousands through the minds of children, transferring my values and imparting not just bookish knowledge, but practical, real—life wisdom to my students. To some of my students, I became a constant, unwavering source of support. To others, I became a powerhouse of encouragement, empowering them to reach new heights. And to those with fragile heart, I became a gentle pillow, a comforting presence where they could cry, share their deepest fear and feel safe from judgment. With these roles to play, I successfully guided my students to rediscover their footing, correcting course for those who were misdirected, lost or simply needed a nudge in the right direction.

As I navigate the twist and turns of my journey. In the pursuit of personal growth, I've come to embrace the philosophy that one must grow with grace, stumble with purpose, and rise with wisdom – for every misstep is a lesson in becoming. It reminds us that personal growth is a continuous process, one that requires efforts, dedication and willingness to learn from our mistakes.

My aspiration is to live a life that is characterized by simplicity, humbleness and deep sense of connection to the world around me. I am drawn to the concept of living in the present, and cultivating a sense of mindfulness that allows me to appreciate the intricate nuances of life.

As I reflect on the memories that I have created thus far, I am filled with a sense of pride and accomplishment. I think back on the moments that have defined me. The experiences that have shaped me and the emotional bonding that have enriched me. And yet, I'm also aware that the true measure of my life will not be in the accumulation of wealth, status or power, but in the positive impact that I have had on the lives of those around me. As I say it to my students "Let your words flow like a river –

calm, clear, and purposeful. Noise may echo, but wisdom endures".

In the end, it is not the grand gesture or the bold declarations that will define my legacy, but the small, everyday act of kindness, compassion that I have shared with others. I just wish that when I reach the final chapter of my life, this story, struggles, challenges that I have overcome with unwavering commitment to living authentically will inspire at least one person to forge a better tomorrow.

The universe operates on a profound principle where every thought, emotion, and action triggers a resonant effect, echoing back to us with precision. This cosmic law, aptly described as the Law of Attraction or Karma, reveals that the vibrational frequency we emit is mirrored back to us, creating a symphony of experiences that shape our reality. But this is partially true; our karma boosts our mind with thoughts that balances our actions (good or bad).

When we engage in selfless acts that uplift others, our minds respond by cultivating even more positive thoughts, propelling us toward growth, healing, and transformation. This virtuous cycle elevates us to become better versions of ourselves, attracting experiences that nurture our soul. Conversely, when our actions cause harm or suffering to others, the universe orchestrates a balancing act, placing us in situations that mirror the pain we've inflicted. This reflective experience invites us to confront the heartache we've caused, fostering empathy, compassion, and personal growth. Through this cosmic dance, we're reminded that every action has a ripple effect, influencing not only our own journey but also the lives of those around us.

In this grand equation of existence, the mind is both soil and seed — absorbing what we feed it and reflecting it back in the form of our reality. When we nourish it with wisdom, compassion, and clarity, it blossoms into a sanctuary of strength. But when we allow it to be cluttered with cynicism, fear, and noise, it withers under the weight of its own confusion. The principle is simple, yet profound: what we consume, we become. Every thought we entertain, every emotion we dwell in, every experience we internalize — they shape the

architecture of our inner world. And so, by choosing to surround ourselves with empowering narratives, soulful connections, and purposeful pursuits, we don't just elevate our mindset — we redefine our destiny. The garden of the mind, when tended with care, becomes a landscape of limitless possibility.
Conversely, when we absorb toxic thoughts, negative self–talk, or harmful influences, our lives can become chaotic, deteriorating to a lower state of being. Our minds transform into barren landscapes, where fear, doubt, and anxiety take root.

By being mindful of the energies we absorb and emit, we can harness the power of this universal law to; Manifest our desires, shape our reality, live a life of intention, purpose, and joy. Create a magnetic field of positivity that attracts abundance and prosperity

As (Bhagavad Gita, Chapter 2, Verse 47) says

"कर्मण्येवाधिकारस्ते मा फलेषु कदाचन।

मा कर्मफलहेतुर्भूर्मा ते सङ्गोऽस्त्वकर्मणि॥"

You have a right to perform your actions, but for the results, you have no control. Never consider yourself the cause of the results of your actions, and never be attached to not doing your duty.

This verse emphasizes that it's not what happens to us, but how we respond to it that truly matters. It encourages us to focus on our actions and reactions, rather than getting caught up in outcomes beyond our control.

By choosing to nourish our minds with positivity, resilience, and determination, we can transform our lives into masterpieces of triumph and fulfillment.

So, let us embark on this extraordinary journey of self—discovery, where we consciously curate the energies we allow into our lives. Let us become the architects of our reality, designing a life that is a testament to the power of positivity, intention, and the unwavering law of attraction.

In conclusion, the universe's karmic law is unequivocal: our actions have consequences that return to us. As the ancient saying goes 'As you sow, so shall you reap.' By embracing this concept, we have to cultivate a deeper sense of responsibility, empathy and wisdom.

'May the ripples of our action return to us as waves of wisdom, guiding us towards a sea of serenity and self–discovery'.

“यथा वृक्षस्य बीजानि, तथा कर्मणां फलानि।

आत्मनि शान्तिमाप्नोति, सन्निधौ लयमाप्नोति।।”

www.ingramcontent.com/pod-product-compliance
Lightning Source LLC
Chambersburg PA
CBHW062106160726
48282CB00026B/690
9789334447668